WINNERS AND LOSERS

COLLECTED STORIES

Charles F. Rechlin

www.beachhousebooks.com

BeachHouse Books
Chesterfield Missouri

Copyright

Graphics Credits:
The cover design is by Dr. Bud Banis based on a stock photograph
from Hemera Photo Clip Art Collection. The photograph of the
author is by Yvonne Bynum.
The illustrations in this collection are by Gregory D. Storey.
ISBN 1-59630-002-7 BeachHouse Books Edition
ISBN 1-59630-003-5 MacroPrintBooks Edition (large print)
Publication date 2005

Library of Congress Cataloging-in-Publication Data
Rechlin, Charles F.
  Winners and losers : collected stories / Charles F. Rechlin.
     p. cm.
  ISBN 1-59630-002-7 (regular print Beachhouse Books : alk.
paper) -- ISBN 1-59630-003-5 (lg. print MacroprintBooks : alk.
paper)
  1. Lawyers--Fiction. 2. Stockbrokers--Fiction. 3. Humorous
fiction. gsafd I. Title.
  PS3618.E423W56 2006
  813'.6--dc22   2006006009

BeachHouse
Books

www.beachhousebooks.com

an Imprint of
Science & Humanities Press
PO Box 7151
Chesterfield, MO 63006-7151
(636) 394-4950
sciencehumanitiespress.com

ACKNOWLEDGEMENTS

Many of the stories in this collection previously appeared (in first-person form) in *Wild Child Magazine.com* under the title *The Education of Stanley Whitehead: Reminiscences of a White Shoe Lawyer*. In addition, the following stories (or versions thereof) previously appeared in the literary publications indicated: "The Cyber Vigilante" in *The Dana Literary Society Online Journal*; "A Day in the Life of Mitchell A. Palmer: White Collar Crime Fighter" in *FAYRDAW*; "The Copywriter" in *The Dana Literary Society Online Journal*; "A Place Apart" in *Words of Wisdom*; "Celebrity" in *The Tenacity Times*; "A Death in the Family" in *Potpourri*; "The Wizard of Wall Street (A Fable of Finance)" in *Wild Child Magazine.com*; "A Man's World" in *Northern Stars Magazine*; "Garbage In, Garbage Out" in *PKA's Advocate* and *Northern Stars Magazine*; "Intervention" in *Abundance Press*; "The Boss" in *Lines in the Sand, Northern Stars Magazine* and *Penny-A-Liner*; "Share and Share Alike" in *Wild Child Magazine.com*; "The Beasts and the Children" in *FAYRDAW*; "The Revolving Door" in *FAYRDAW*; "Prohibition" in *Vermont Ink*; "The Right Place" in *The Tenacity Times*; "The Busybody" in *Vermont Ink*; "Role Model" in *Northern Stars Magazine*; and "The Grandfather Clock" in *The Oak*.

STORIES

NEW YORK STORIES

THE CYBER VIGILANTE

"I always suspected," he observed to himself, "that an investment banker and a second-story man had a great deal in common."

Thorne Smith, *The Stray Lamb*

Growing up, Terry Turner dreamed of one day working on Wall Street. While boyhood chums aspired to be athletes or rock stars, worshiping the likes of Joe Montana and Mick Jagger, young Terry—son of an internist who spent more time on the phone to his stockbroker than ministering to the sick—longed to become a financial titan, following in the gilded footsteps of J.P. Morgan and Bernard Baruch. Already, as an awkward and introverted teenager, an avid reader of *Barron's*, *Business Week* and *Fortune*, Terry would imagine himself at the center of big deals, revered in financial circles. He'd fantasize about living in Manhattan, inhabiting penthouse digs overlooking the Hudson, whisked around in a stretch limo, entertaining the movers and shakers of American enterprise at Delmonico's and Twenty-One, and escorting buxom beauties to Broadway openings and home games at the Garden.

But, sadly, at age twenty-five, Terry's youthful dreams lay in tatters. Employed, not as a financial deal-maker, but as a night word processor at a downtown law firm, and living, not in a luxury Westside condo, but in an Eighth Street walk-up, Terry found himself shut out of Wall Street, spurned by the professional training programs of every firm he'd applied to.

"What did you expect?" taunted his long-time girlfriend, Janet DeMarco, as he showed her his latest rejection

3

letter—from Drexel, Birnbaum—which, while commending "your candor about your utter lack of financial experience," nevertheless suggested that "you continue to pursue your promising career in word processing." "Graduating at the bottom of your class at Hunter didn't help! If you hadn't spent so much time fooling around with your computer, and buckled down to your studies, maybe you'd of gotten into business school."

Stung by Janet's rebuke, Terry tried to defend himself. "That's not fair," he protested. "I'm ... well ... different ... special. I've always been honest and played by the rules. But I guess, to Wall Street, that makes me an outsider."

"'Outsider'?" the salty red-head shrieked in disbelief. "Don't you know you're sitting on a pot of gold?"

The scrawny, bespectacled Terry stared blankly at his girlfriend.

"Do I have to spell everything out for you?" she huffed. "Listen, Einstein. As a word processor at a fat cat law firm, you could clean up. Probably every night you type some document oozing with inside information. You could make millions off it."

Terry's jaw dropped. "Are you suggesting that I ... er ... engage in insider trading?" he stammered. "I could go to jail for that!"

"So what? All I know is it's done every day. And, in my book, it's okay as long as you don't get caught. Besides, I'd rather see you rotting in the slammer than moping around here, whining like a kid beaten senseless by the neighborhood bully."

That afternoon, taking the subway to work, Terry felt like a marathoner in a race in which the judges keep moving back the finish line. He saw himself as the victim of a gross

4

injustice, wrongfully denied the career he'd aspired to because of his own honesty.

Getting off at William Street, his eye caught the headline

"HACKER SHUTS DOWN DREXEL, BIRNBAUM: THE STRANGE CASE OF THE 'POISON E-MAIL': Story on Page Three."

on that afternoon's *Post*:

Purchasing the tabloid, Terry leaned against a nearby dumpster and read the article inside.

"Business at Wall Street powerhouse Drexel, Birnbaum ground to a halt today as an e-mail virus disabled the company's computer network. The e-mail, headed 'Thanks for Nothing' and dispatched by a hacker styling himself 'The Avenger,' transmitted an unknown virus that caused stock prices to be misquoted, changed 'buy' orders into 'sell' orders and 'sell' orders into 'buy' orders, and otherwise disrupted transactions at the prestigious brokerage firm for hours.

"Although the identity of the hacker remains a mystery, sources speculate that the toxic message may have been sent by a dissatisfied customer, or disgruntled job seeker . . . ."

Suddenly, Terry had an idea—a way of getting back at those who had rejected him. If he couldn't buy and sell stocks on inside information, maybe he could get Wall Street traders to buy and sell—and lose their shirts in the process—by sending out his own toxic messages over the Internet. Where the facts in his possession indicated that a stock should be bought, he'd recommend a sale; where the facts indicated that a stock should be sold, he'd recommend a buy. And he could do it all from cyberspace.

During his dinner break, Terry tapped into the computer network of Prudent Securities, the firm's biggest brokerage client. Once inside, he obtained the confidential Web addresses and secret passwords of Internet chat rooms dedicated exclusively to professional stock traders, where investment hotshots gathered to exchange lucrative scuttlebutt, swapping tips, rumors and buzz about stocks. To disguise his identity, he also lifted the names and social security, credit card and telephone numbers of a dozen or so Prudent Securities clients from its customer records.

"Who do you think you are—Charles Bronson?" scoffed Janet when Terry revealed his plans the next day. "Sounds pretty goofy to me!"

But Terry didn't care what Janet thought. He was ready to take on Wall Street.

~ ~

Terry struck first at that bastion of professional trading—the Masters of the Universe Chat Room

(Address: www.coiningmoney.com;

Password: midastouch).

Logging on as WIZZKID22, he had no difficulty penetrating the privileged sanctuary.

At first, Terry planted tidbits of genuine information, hoping to lure his victims into a trap. He recommended the purchase of Utensils 'R Us, revealing that he'd been told by "inside sources" that the company would soon split its stock and increase its dividend (which he knew from typing a proposed press release at his firm). He followed up by trumpeting Amalgabanc, citing, from "people in the know," a plan to slash expenses by laying off 1,500 white collar workers (which he learned about from an internal memo written by a firm labor lawyer). Traders relying upon Terry's information profited handsomely.

Before long, Terry was the darling of the chat room crowd, particularly of its moderator, a trader identifying himself only as IOU2000.

IOU2000: Hey, WIZZKID22, got any sure things—any inside dope?

WIZZKID22: Not today. But I'm working on something big!

IOU2000: We'll be here—same time, same station.

That evening, Terry typed a draft agreement—marked "SUPER SECRET, EYES ONLY"—for the merger of a company code-named "Alpha" with a company code-named "Omega." In his apparent haste to complete the document, the young lawyer involved had neglected to use the code names in several places, inadvertently identifying the actual parties. His oversight gave Terry the ammunition he needed.

The next day, ensconced behind his pc like a camouflaged machine gunner, Terry unloaded.

WIZZKID22: I hear Business Computing Systems is about to announce a glitch in its latest spreadsheet software. Sounds like a good candidate to sell short.

IOU2000: I've already got my trading desk on the line . . . .

The resulting carnage was reported in the next day's *Wall Street Journal*:

"Prominent stock traders declined comment on yesterday's unprecedented 'short squeeze' in shares of Business Computing Systems following its surprise announcement that it would be acquired by Marvel Software Co. for $50 a share. Prior to the announcement, BCS plummeted from

$30 to $15 a share as an unexplained wave of short selling hit the stock. After the announcement, the price soared to over $80, as befuddled investors scrambled to cover their shorts . . . ."

Yet, despite the rout, when Terry logged into the chat room that morning (under the new name BullyBoy), no one would admit to having lost money on the bogus tip.

IOU2000: Did you hear how some fools got burned on BCS? WIZZKID22 doesn't know his ass from a hole in the ground. I assume no one in this room got hosed!

[11 answers]: Not me.

IOU2000: Say, where is WIZZKID22?

Despite this lack of recognition, Terry continued pedaling misinformation like a vendor of aluminum siding hawking his wares from the back of a pickup. During the following weeks, he: under the name GoofyGuy, touted Pharout Pharmaceuticals in the Prime Brokers War Room (aware, from a confidential letter he'd typed, of the clinical failure of a much ballyhooed experimental drug); posing as mrstreet, recommended, on the electronic bulletin board of Stock Pickers Anonymous, that investors hold onto Eat 'N Run Restaurants, ignoring insolvency rumors (which, having seen a draft of the bankruptcy papers, he knew were accurate); and, adopting the handle MONEYMAN, suggested that those occupying the Broad Street Barracks sell short Golfco immediately prior to a management buy-out announcement (which he gleaned from piecing together a word processing document fished out of a firm shredder).

Terry calculated that, by this point, his misinformation campaign must have caused tens of millions in trading losses. Yet, each time he struck, the reaction was the same: no one would admit to having taken a hit.

~ ~

"I don't understand," Terry complained to Janet one day, as the two sat having coffee at Starbuck's. "I've scammed the biggest traders on the Street, but they won't admit it. I'm still an outsider!"

"Don't be so naive," Janet retorted. "Stock traders would never confess to being duped. It would destroy their public images."

"You mean they'll never admit I've bamboozled them?"

Janet threw a packet of Nutra Sweet at her boyfriend. "Good guess, Aristotle!"

"But isn't there anything I can do?"

A devious smile crossed the young woman's face. "Well, I hate to use the word 'blackmail' . . . ."

Terry abruptly raised his hand. "Hold it right there. I don't want to hear what you're about to suggest."

"Pipe down," Janet snarled. "I mean, what's wrong with a little extortion? Just tell these chat room types that, if they don't give you what you want, you'll spill the beans about their losses to Louis Rukhyser—or whoever it is you leak stuff like that to."

"But what do I want?"

"I dunno. How about ten million dollars—for starters?"

"Janet, I don't even know who these people are. They're just numbers and letters on a computer screen. Besides, I could never bring myself to . . . to . . . ."

"Spit it out, lover. To what? To stand up for yourself? To be a man? For once in your life, use your head!"

Stunned, Terry bolted from the restaurant. "I don't want to hear any more of this!" he muttered as he ran down the street to the subway station.

~ ~

Terry pulled off more hoaxes, but nothing changed. As long as his victims refused to recognize him, the personal satisfaction of revenge was illusory.

To pacify Janet, he drafted an extortion threat to post on bulletin boards. But it sounded more like an apology than a blackmail note. The reticent word processor couldn't bring himself to demand money — or anything else, for that matter. The young man who'd always known what he wanted now wasn't sure what he wanted.

Then, one afternoon, passing the subway newsstand on his way to work, Terry noticed a startling headline in the *Post*.

"WALL STREET TAKES A HIT! DOW JONES AVERAGE PLUMMETS 3,500 POINTS AS MASSIVE CORPORATE FRAUD UNCOVERED. INVESTORS STUNNED BY REVELATIONS."

As ashen-faced office workers passed by, Terry sat on the grimy stone stairway and read the details.

"It seems that investors have been taken for chumps, led astray by one corporate management after another. 'If you can't believe a company's numbers,' one shell-shocked shareholder asked, 'what can you believe?' At this moment, it is unclear whether our nation's financial markets will ever recover from these revelations of widespread corporate wrongdoing."

After calling in sick from a pay phone, Terry rushed home to tell Janet about the crash. Now, he'd no longer have to pursue his vendetta against Wall Street. The stock traders he so despised had been punished enough — and by the very insiders they so avidly courted.

But, when he arrived at the apartment, Janet was gone. Pasted to his computer screen was a Post-It Note:

"Dear Terry,
"I'm tired of waiting for you to grow up. I'm going back to Hoboken.
     Goodbye,
     Janet
P. S. I think your vigilante scheme is nutty. For your own good, I broke into the chat rooms and posted your name and number on their bulletin boards."

Looking up through mist-filled eyes, Terry saw the message light blinking on his answering machine.

"Son, what's it going to take to buy you off?" asked IOU2000 when Terry returned his call.

In the background, Terry heard shouting on a trading floor. "Dump that crap!" "Sell that sucker!"

"Why would you buy me off — *now*?" he asked incredulously. "Weren't you wiped out in the crash?"

Derisive laughter burst from the receiver. "Kid, don't you know anything?" the trader cackled. "Guys like us always hedge our bets. When someone says buy, we load up on puts; when they say sell, we buy up every call in

11

sight. We're invincible, in good markets and bad. Hell, I had so many puts on the Dow Jones Average that I actually made money today!"

"Then, you didn't lose anything on the bad tips I gave you?"

"Hell, no. After all, you can't believe everything you hear. That's why I'm a professional—and you're not."

"Why do you care about me, then?"

"Because you're getting in the way. We traders would just as soon not have rank amateurs like you around, gumming up the works. And we're willing to pay you to go away—and stay away."

"What are you offering?"

"Two million bucks—no questions asked. You just leave our chat rooms and don't come back."

Terry hesitated. "Gee, I'm really not interested in money. But I'm not sure what I want. Let me get back to you."

"The sooner, the better." The trader paused. "And, son . . . ."

"Yes?"

"Just remember—you've got a lot to learn!"

That fall, Terry entered Harvard Business School. He was admitted, despite his poor college record, based on the recommendations of several prominent stock traders in New York.

"Oh, Terry, I can't wait until you start that big job you've been promised at General Motors," cooed Terry's new significant other, Stella Duncan, as the two strolled hand-in-hand in Harvard Yard one sunny Indian summer afternoon. "It will be the fulfillment of your dreams."

Terry scratched his head. "I don't know, Stella. I'm having second thoughts about Detroit. There are so many other things I could do. I'm even thinking of going back to New York—maybe trade stocks on Wall Street . . . ."

"Are you sure you want to do that?" asked Stella, wide-eyed. "You know how cutthroat Wall Street is. I'm not sure you're suited for it—you're so . . . so . . . sensitive."

Terry laughed. "It's really not as bad as you think, Stella. Besides, I've grown up a lot recently. Somehow, I have the feeling I could make quite a killing in the market."

Gazing up at the clear blue sky, Terry smiled wistfully. "Yes," he said, squeezing Stella's hand tightly in his, "a real killing!"

A DAY IN THE LIFE OF MITCHELL A. PALMER: WHITE COLLAR CRIME FIGHTER

Mitchell A. Palmer, Deputy State's Attorney for White Collar and Victimless Crime, sat in his musty Centre Street office, his feet up on his rickety metal desk, his arms folded across his chest, gazing idly out his dirt-streaked window at the gridlocked cross-town traffic. Before the portly prosecutor sat a half-eaten jelly donut, an unopened carton of lukewarm orange juice and a Styrofoam cup filled with stale, reheated coffee. Although only nine-thirty, the temperature in downtown Manhattan had already soared past eighty degrees, and Palmer, jacket off, shirt sleeves rolled up, collar unbuttoned and tie untied, was bathed in sweat. Beneath the desk, in the darkness, a family of cockroaches, foraging for food, stirred uneasily.

Palmer sat up abruptly and rapped his chubby knuckles on the desktop, calling his regular Monday morning staff meeting to order. The staff, consisting of Vernon Vassal — chief investigator — and Lisa Dolittle — paralegal, stenographer, word processor and file clerk — sat awkwardly before him in battered folding chairs. Palmer began by asking for an update on the ongoing probe of WIZKID22 a/k/a HOTSHOT1 a/k/a StockBoy a/k/a Goofyguy a/k/a mrstreet — the elusive "Cyber Felon."

"Gee wizz, boss," the gaunt young investigator replied, his Adam's apple bobbing up and down like an errant ping-pong ball, "shouldn't we be discussing the rash of corporate fraud instead? I mean, the stock market nose-dived Friday. Small investors are getting wiped out. And all because of management corruption and dishonesty.

15

Why waste any more time on a nut case like the Cyber Felon?"

The prosecutor glowered at his subordinate. "Because," he bellowed, "we work the Wall Street beat! Our job is to root out and punish crooked stockbrokers and traders, not lying, cheating CEOs and CFOs. Now, where do we stand on the Cyber Felon?"

The chastened Vassal continued. "Well, he struck again last week. On Monday, he broke into the Financial Wizards Chatroom on the Interlog Network, touting Technicorp stock. Then, on Wednesday, he infiltrated the SuperBrokers Forum on US Online, bashing Enerco."

"With the usual results?" Palmer asked matter-of-factly.

"Yes sir. On Tuesday, Technicorp announced that it was filing for bankruptcy. After the close on Wednesday, Enerco disclosed that it was being acquired by MEGA Ltd. — at twice market."

"Fascinating," remarked the veteran prosecutor, extracting a deposit of dirt from under a fingernail with the tip of a ballpoint pen. "Instead of trading on inside information for profit, like anyone in his right mind would do, the Cyber Felon uses inside information to screw people. *He gets his victims to do exactly the opposite of what they should do!* He makes them think black is white, and white is black. What's this bozo after, anyway? A one-way ticket to Belleview?"

"I dunno, chief," answered Vassal, reaching into his briefcase and retrieving a crumpled sheaf of papers. "But we've been inundated with complaints from professional stock traders. Just look at these letters . . . ."

Palmer raised his hand disdainfully. "Don't bother me with that crap. I'm not interested in reading self-serving drivel. But tell me, exactly who are these so-called 'professional stock traders'?"

16

"Well, boss, most of the complainants are big-time stock market speculators in New York, Boston, Chicago and LA—prima donnas with eight-figure incomes and egos to match. But, for security reasons, we're calling them 'John Doe,' 'Jane Doe,' 'Richard Roe,' et cetera. The Big Guy—I mean, the State's Attorney—kinda promised them confidentiality—you know, like rape victims get."

Palmer emitted a ferocious belly-laugh, in the process knocking his coffee over on his tattered desk blotter. The roaches scrambled for cover as a torrent of rancid liquid rained onto the scuffed linoleum floor.

"How appropriate!" Palmer chortled, wiping up the mess with a copy of that morning's *Daily News*. "But it figures. Those financial wizards don't want anyone to know they've been duped by some computer nerd. It wouldn't square with their public image as Masters of the Universe. I'm glad they're losing their shirts! Serves 'em right!"

Vassal nervously cleared his throat. "Actually boss, they haven't really lost anything. You see, professional traders always hedge their bets. What they're complaining about is . . . er . . . lost opportunities . . . ."

"Lost opportunities! Don't those crooks make enough money already?"

Just then, a clattering sound filled the room, followed by a prolonged groan, a series of short coughs, a weak rattle and then silence.

"There it goes again!" grumbled Palmer. "When are they going to fix the damn air conditioning around here?"

Lisa Dolittle squirmed in her seat. The shapely young brunette, her hair done up in a mountainous bouffant, crossed her legs, removed a wad of chewing gum from her mouth and affixed it to the underside of her chair.

"Probably never, Mr. Palmer," she said. "It seems we can't afford anything in this office. 'Budgetary problems,' they say—'a resource dilemma.' Like, the chintzy Purchasing Department won't even spring for a lousy pc. I mean, how can anyone expect us to fight white collar crime when we don't even have a desktop? Why, when I was at Allen & White, everybody had one—even the janitor . . . ."

The beleaguered lawman scowled. "That's enough, Ms. Dolittle! You can't compare working here with working at one of those fat-cat downtown law firms. That's like comparing Saint Patrick's Cathedral to a crack house in Bedford Stuyvesant."

"I'm sorry, Mr. Palmer," the paralegal said contritely. "It's just that—well—I think it would be nice if we had a few modern conveniences around the office, that's all. Sometimes this place seems so . . . so . . . *Dickensian!*"

The prosecutor started at this display of erudition on the part of the secretary. "Very true, Ms. Dolittle," he replied. "Nevertheless, we just have to make due with what we've got. For example, can't we use the mainframe to track down the Cyber Felon?"

"I'm afraid not, boss," answered Vassal glumly. "It's down for repairs. Our technology isn't exactly state-of-the art. In fact, we're still trying to fix the Millennium Bug."

"But the Millennium's come and gone, Vernon!"

"I know, boss. We're a little behind schedule."

Palmer rose and began pacing back and forth, a bleak expression on his bloated face. "We need help," he grunted. "Big time."

Waiting for the central operator to place the call to Washington, Palmer gazed nostalgically at a faded photograph on his desk. Taken fifteen years before at the annual awards dinner of the Association of Public Prosecutors at the Waldorf Astoria, it showed Palmer—his light gray hair tousled, his enormous gut spilling out over his trousers, his suit jacket two sizes too small—accepting a silver plaque honoring his years of public service from a gaunt, hollow-cheeked man in spectacles with a ferocious demeanor. The photograph was inscribed: "To Mitch—The Enforcer's Enforcer—Thanks for everything and the best of luck—Rudy Giuliani." Rudy—now there was a prosecutor!

The rotary phone rang. Palmer grabbed the receiver.

"Mr. Palmer, sir," came the nasal voice of the operator, "I have Mr. Bastion from the Federal Securities Bureau on the line. Go ahead, Mr. Bastion."

"Mitch, I hope you're not calling about that damn Cyber Felon case of yours again," bellowed Clinton Bastion, the Acting Deputy Chief of Enforcement of the FSB, without even bothering to say "hello." "I've already told you we can't handle it just now."

Palmer self-consciously cleared his throat. "Well, as a matter of fact, Clint, I was. It strikes me that it's an ideal case for you fellows down in Washington . . . ."

"Mitch, how many times do I have to say 'no' to you? Right now, our entire staff is trying to get a handle on this outbreak of corporate fraud. In case you didn't notice, the stock market dropped thirty-five hundred points on Friday!"

"Well, what about Justice?" Palmer persisted, ignoring Bastion's professional swipe. "Can they take this on?"

"No way. They're in the same position we are. We've all got more important things to do than tracking down some psycho who gets his kicks playing head games with stock market speculators."

Palmer shook his head and sighed. "Well, do you have any bright ideas about what I should do?"

"Apart from giving up your investigation — no. But you might think about something. Have you ever considered whether the Cyber Felon is some sort of vigilante? You know, like Charles Bronson? Maybe someone with a grudge against Wall Street."

Palmer roared with laughter. "Clint, if this guy's Charles Bronson, then my mother's the Zodiac Killer! This isn't Hollywood."

"Well, I was only trying to be helpful."

Palmer shifted about uncomfortably in his squeaky swivel chair. He wished he could reach into the phone and grab the young bureaucrat by the throat.

"You've been about as helpful as a migraine!" he barked, slamming down the receiver.

Palmer buried his head in his hands and pondered his next move.

~ ~

"Mitch, don't take it personally. The hiring freeze is affecting all of us. The Legislature slashed our funding ten percent, and there's nothing we can do about it. And, what with the market plunge last week, we'll probably be cut back even more! You can't squeeze blood out of a turnip."

Palmer sat on the thread-bare sofa in the State's Attorney's office. The law enforcement chief — an ambitious, mustached young man fifteen years Palmer's junior, currently cultivating the spiffy, groom-on-the-wedding cake appearance of Thomas E. Dewey — was explaining why his request for two new staff investigators had been denied.

"But I need more bodies, boss," Palmer pleaded. "There's an epidemic of white collar crime on Wall Street:

20

bucket shop and boiler room swindles that would turn your stomach—an infestation of fraud and bunko the likes of which we've never seen before!"

The State's Attorney shook his head. "If you ask me, Mitch, the only infestation we have is the vermin that have taken up residence in our offices. (You don't know a good exterminator, do you?) Anyway, I think you're going a bit overboard . . . ."

Palmer's face turned a bright red. "No way, boss. If I had the tools I needed, I could rid this city of these financial crooks and con men—with their Mercedes and Porsches, their fancy summer homes in the Hamptons, their bloated bank accounts—practically overnight. Take this Cyber Felon case, for instance . . . ."

The State's Attorney put his arm around his deputy's shoulders. "Calm down, Mitch—there's no use getting excited. If I didn't know better, I'd say you were pursuing some sort of personal vendetta against the financial community."

The prosecutor turned away, feigning shock at his superior's suggestion. "Boss, how could you say that? After all my years of public service . . . ."

"Don't take it personally, my friend," the young official consoled his subordinate. "I know how hard it can be sometimes—feeling neglected, unwanted, unappreciated. But we in government have to learn to get along with those we regulate. We should be kinder and gentler with Wall Street, particularly now that it's suffered such staggering losses at the hands of unscrupulous corporate wrongdoers. Oh, sure, these people have made mistakes along the way. But, Mitch, nobody's perfect! In tough times, we should be partners with those in the financial community, not their adversaries. In fact, I've taken a very significant step in that direction. I've just accepted an invitation from three major investment banking firms to join the Downtowners

Club as a lifetime member. Imagine that! Pretty good for a kid from Garden City!"

Palmer gazed at his boss in disbelief, his mouth agape. He suddenly felt nauseous.

"Anyway, we're not living in the Greedy Eighties and Naughty Nineties anymore. This is the Information Age, Mitch — the New Millennium. You need a more enlightened approach to law enforcement!"

What a gasbag, Palmer thought to himself as he fled his boss's office and went to lunch.

After wolfing down a half-cooked hamburger, a container of cold, soggy French fries and a can of warm diet soda at his desk, Palmer suffered an attack of acute indigestion. He scrambled to the men's room, seeking refuge in the handicapped stall. With him he carried his coffee-stained copy of the *Daily News* and Vernon Vassal's secret list of the complainants in the Cyber Felon case.

Squatting on the raised toilet seat, Palmer glanced at the

"PARENT SLAYER CLAIMS CHILDHOOD ABUSE, ASSERTS SELF-DEFENSE," "THWARTED SUICIDE WINS $1 MILLION VERDICT AGAINST MTA FOR NEGLIGENT OPERATION OF SUBWAY," "FREEWAY SHOOTING VICTIM JAILED FOR DRIVING WITHOUT LICENSE," "PTA PRESIDENT 'OUTED' AS CLOSET LESBIAN."

lead headlines in the tabloid:

(The Friday market crash was not mentioned until page 20.) Palmer tore up the paper in disgust He then turned his attention to the victims of the Cyber Felon. The list was a virtual *Who's Who* of financial big shots — stock traders, investment bankers and money managers who'd for years cleaned up on Wall Street, regularly manipulating the system to their exclusive advantage. Honest prosecutors like Palmer had never been able to pin anything on these pros. They didn't have the evidence.

How ironic, thought Palmer, that these career con men were now treated as "victims." Who were the real criminals, he mused, and who were their prey? Clint Bastion's question began to haunt him: "Have you ever considered whether the Cyber Felon is some sort of vigilante . . . . Maybe someone with a grudge against Wall Street?"

Suddenly, Palmer knew what he had to do.

When Lisa Dolittle entered Palmer's office, she found her boss crouching down behind his desk, a flashlight in one hand and a can of Raid in the other. A foul odor filled the air.

"Finally nailed those buggers," he proclaimed, pointing the secretary to four shriveled-up cockroach carcasses floating in a pool of white liquid underneath the desk. "Thought they could get away. But I showed 'em!"

"Mr. Palmer, you wanted me to take dictation?" the secretary asked nervously.

"Oh, yes, Ms. Dolittle. Please have a seat."

Palmer stared out the window at the street below. "The People," he sighed. "So vulnerable, so helpless — like tiny insects scurrying around, about to be crushed underfoot by thugs in $1,000 Italian suits and $200 wing-tip shoes. Ms. Dolittle, it is our sworn duty to protect them — to bring the white collar criminals to justice!"

Palmer turned back from the window and began pacing the floor, an almost messianic fire in his eyes. "Take a memo, Ms. Dolittle — to the State's Attorney — re the Cyber Felon."

The secretary collapsed into a chair. Palmer began dictating.

"After an agonizing reappraisal, I have reluctantly concluded that this office should cease further investigation into the matter of the so-called 'Cyber Felon.' It has become painfully obvious that we cannot track down and prosecute this computer criminal. Without the cooperation of the so-called 'victims,' adequate investigative tools and the assistance of other law enforcement agencies, further pursuit of the Cyber Felon would be futile. Dropping the case would also be consistent with our new policy of enlightened law enforcement — of our kinder, gentler approach to those we regulate."

"Mr. Palmer," the assistant exclaimed, "how can you drop this case? I mean, it's not like you to give up so easily. What about our mission of bringing Wall Street criminals to justice?"

Palmer smiled benignly. "Ms. Dolittle, that's exactly what I propose to do. I'm going to shine the light of justice on the wrongdoers!"

Just then, Vernon Vassal entered the office. "Boss," he said breathlessly. "I just got a call from one of the traders saying they're dropping their complaints against the Cyber Felon. Looks like we can call off our investigation . . . ."

Palmer raised his hand. "Not yet, Vernon," he said calmly. "Justice remains to be done. Now, I have a small favor to ask. As you know, we are living in the Information Age . . . ."

24

~ ~

Mitchell A. Palmer left his office late that evening. There was so much work to be done, and so little time to do it.

As he strode to the parking garage through the muggy evening air, he stopped off at a newsstand and bought the early edition of the *Daily News*. He beamed as he read the front page headline:

> "FINANCIAL BIG SHOTS DUPED BY COMPUTER NERD—
> SAVVY INVESTORS TAKEN IN BY HIGH-TECH HIT MAN—
> 'Are You Interested in Buying a Bridge?—I've Got One Cheap'—
> Names and Other Details Inside."

Folding the paper under his arm, Palmer jauntily strolled to his car, satisfied that, at long last, justice had been done.

THE COPYWRITER

At Fordham, they taught Wayne Zeminsky that a law degree was a license to do good. "You've been empowered!" crowed Anita Oglethorpe, the feisty but graying Professor of Environmental, Poverty and Gender Bias Law, addressing Wayne's class of newly-minted attorneys as they assembled to collect their hard-earned sheepskins. "Now, it's up to you to make the world a better place." Wayne believed every word.

Four years, three jobs and two wives later, his youthful ardor dissipated like squandered lotto winnings, a dispirited Wayne listened in stony silence while his headhunter described "the only interview I could get for a guy like you."

"Copywriter?" Wayne finally said. "Writing fine print? What kind of job is that?"

There was a brief pause. "The only kind available," the headhunter replied matter-of-factly. "Face it, Wayne, you're not cut out to be a lawyer. First, you washed out of the Public Defender's office, then the Bureau of Consumer Affairs. And your performance at that public interest law firm — what did they call themselves, the Big Green Legal Machine? — was, to say the least, less than stellar. I couldn't even get you in to see Legal Aid!"

Stunned, Wayne pondered his brief, unspectacular career at the Bar — the forgotten deadlines, tardy court appearances, mislaid files, rebukes from judges and clients about his inattention to detail, disorganization and lack of focus. Now, flat broke and committed to supporting second wife Thelma's foray into the world of modern art, he was bereft of options.

The next morning, donning an old brown suit, crumpled white shirt, frayed blue necktie and non-matching socks, the gaunt ex-attorney stumbled from his West Village walk-up and took the subway to the Madison Avenue headquarters of Bolen, Barker, Byers and Bigalow, Ltd., advertising and public relations.

"I admit it's not glamorous work," chortled Bruce Byers, BBB&B's svelte, silver-haired Vice Chairman, as the two met in his twenty-ninth floor office, "but somebody's got to do it. And, with your legal background . . . ."

As Byers soliloquized about the "advertising game," Wayne slumped uneasily in an oversized sofa chair, wondering how he'd ever gotten there. "Excuse me, sir," he ventured sheepishly, "I know it's an important position and all that, but what . . . uh . . . er . . . would I be doing—exactly?"

The executive smiled condescendingly. "Son, you'd be performing the most important task in advertising—telling the truth!"

"The truth?" Wayne gulped.

"Let me explain," Byers continued, fixing a stern eye on the youthful job applicant. "As a fine print writer, you'd pen the disclaimers, warnings, exceptions, exclusions, qualifications, conditions, restrictions, limitations, provisos, definitions and other terms that convert our ad copy from so much fluff into the unvarnished truth! You'd put honesty and integrity into every ad!"

After Byers offered him the job on the spot, Wayne had little choice but to accept. When he informed Thelma of his new gig, the frizzy-haired young sculptress (at work in her makeshift studio on a replica of an urban guerilla fabricated entirely of steel wool) reacted with skepticism. "I knew you'd sell out," she observed. "Lawyers always do."

$$\sim \quad \sim$$

To his surprise, Wayne quickly adapted to the job, which he carried on behind a computer screen in a small cubicle within a cavernous, dimly-lit room, along with ten other former attorneys.

Fortunately, it didn't require much talent. Called upon to do no more than mindlessly repeat what he'd been told, Wayne would simply take the advertising copy prepared by the firm's Creative Group, compare it to the actual proposal sent in by the client, then add back, with boilerplate borrowed from other ads, all the important facts that had been omitted. Thus, where a fast-food chain ad trumpeted "$1.99 Happy Mondays," Wayne inserted "available at selected locations for a limited time only"; where a sweepstakes mailer proclaimed "YOU MAY HAVE ALREADY WON $10 MILLION," Wayne footnoted "if your number was selected from over 30 million entries;" and, where an ad for BBB&B's principal client—Wall Street powerhouse United Financial Services—promised "Riches Beyond Your Wildest Dreams," it fell to Wayne to caution that "past performance is not necessarily indicative of future results."

Best of all, the job entailed none of the hassles that had plagued his abbreviated legal career. Gone were the pesky phone calls, endless meetings, intractable time schedules, frantic court appearances, badgering clients, high-handed judges and relentless opposing counsel that had made his life as a lawyer a living Hell. Attention to font, type size and spacing soon replaced anxieties over pleadings, depositions and trials.

Wayne shot up the corporate ladder, rising from "Assistant Copywriter" to "Associate Copywriter" to

"Senior Copywriter" in less than a year. Given all fine print responsibilities for the United Financial account, he seemed to have finally found his niche.

"Just keep on doin' what you're doin'," Byers would encourage him after each promotion and pay raise.

Eventually, however, Wayne began to wonder exactly what he was doing—or at least how he was doing it. Although appreciative of the promotions, pats on the back and friendly admonitions to "stay the course," he found it odd that no one ever commented on his work. Once he finished a task, he'd never hear about it again—from the client, from his bosses, from anyone—even though he'd sometimes overlook a detail here or botch a sentence there. Even when he admitted to a particularly egregious gaff—like using eight-point type instead of six—all he'd ever receive from Byers was a wink and a nod, followed by a perfunctory "nobody's perfect" or "thanks for the heads-up."

"I'm confused," he confessed to Thelma one evening as the two lugged her latest creation—a statue of a Freedom Rider forged out of wire hangers—up the rickety steps of a Bleeker Street loft for her first public showing. "Copywriting isn't like practicing law. Nobody seems to care how I do my job."

The budding artist shook her head. "Wayne, don't be naive. Of course nobody cares. I mean, who ever reads the fine print?"

Wayne dropped his end of Thelma's masterpiece. "But that's where the truth is!"

His wife clucked her tongue. "Lover, only the lawyers know that!"

~ ~

Troubled by Thelma's observation, Wayne tried an experiment. Summoning up all the courage he could muster, he misspelled (in three places) the client's name in a full-page ad for a new United Financial tax shelter product. The copy sailed through editorial, production and printing without notice. When it appeared in *The Wall Street Journal*, Wayne heard not a word of criticism. He was devastated.

"So you're the guy who spelled 'United' U-N-T-I-E-D!" chuckled Jeff Grisham, a Fordham classmate, now a self-styled "private attorney general," specializing in strike suits and class actions against financial conglomerates and multinationals, as the two shared lunch at The Brasserie.

Wayne, who'd invited Grisham to lunch to seek his friend's advice about his floundering advertising career, choked on a piece of broiled salmon.

"You mean you actually read the fine print?" he asked, wiping his tie with a pink table napkin.

The hefty, unkempt Grisham roared with laughter. "Of course. It's my job!"

Wayne explained the circumstances surrounding his dirty trick. "I feel unappreciated . . . worthless!"

The lawyer rolled his eyes. "Worthless! Jesus, you're saving the butts of those fat-cat clients of yours — and killing public interest lawyers like me in the process. You might not be perfect, but you do your job better than most. Because of you and your disclaimers, I can't get a case for fraud or mismanagement past the judge anymore. I'm always getting thrown out of court on my ear!"

Wayne scratched his head, perplexed. "But I thought nobody reads the fine print."

"That's the problem — they don't. The widows and orphans who buy the crap that United Financial pedals don't find out about the fine print until they've lost the

31

family farm and hired lawyers like me to try to get it back. But by then it's too late. Wayne, you're screwing the little people! Whatever happened to your social conscience?"

Revulsion overcame Wayne like exhaust from a Transit Authority bus. He became defensive. "Well, at least I'm telling the truth. That's more than you can say for a lot of lawyers."

The litigator snickered. "Give me a break. As far as I'm concerned, the truth stinks!"

Wayne couldn't sleep that night. As he restlessly paced his apartment, his neglected idealism haunted him like a youthful indiscretion. Had he become a tool of the rich and powerful? Could he really be hurting the ordinary people he'd always championed? Had he no integrity left?

Wandering into Thelma's studio, he stared thoughtfully at her current work-in-progress, a depiction of the Kent State Massacre fabricated from discarded bottles and cans. He'd told her it looked more like a trailer park leveled by a tornado than a representation of militant social protest. Now, however, examining it more carefully, Wayne thought she might be on to something . . . .

The next morning, Wayne called Grisham. "Jeff, you've convinced me I'm doing the Devil's Work. I'm going to quit my job and go back to the law — helping the poor, the downtrodden . . . ."

Grisham cleared his throat. "That's very noble, Wayne. But are you really sure you're cut out to practice law? And, with all you've done for big business, would anyone want you back? Maybe you ought to stay put."

"Isn't there anything I can do to make up for all the harm I've done?"

There was a protracted silence on the line. "Well, maybe *if you did something socially relevant — performed some selfless act . . . .*"

At that moment, Wayne's long-dormant sense of empowerment returned.

~ ~

Wayne sat in Jeff Grisham's well-appointed Park Avenue office, gazing wistfully out the window at the Manhattan skyline, as the lawyer barked into the telephone.

"Tell your client I won't settle for a penny less than $25 million. That whole crowd over at United Financial oughtta be tossed in the slammer for what they've done. Sending out an advertising piece like that! Not telling innocent investors about the risks involved. Talk about fraud! Don't they even read their own fine print? A bunch of gangsters, if you ask me."

Slamming down the receiver, Grisham turned to Wayne, a self-satisfied grin on his face.

"Wayne, my boy," he said, "that was a gutsy thing you did. You're the talk of the plaintiff's bar!"

Wayne shrugged. "Maybe so. But what if my old bosses come after me?"

"They wouldn't dare," Grisham scoffed, planting his feet firmly on his immaculate desk. "It'd be too embarrassing for 'em. Besides, if they did, you'd have your old buddy Jeff Grisham, attorney-at-law, there to defend you."

"But I still don't have a job. What am I going to do for a living now that I've left the advertising business?"

The lawyer wearily rubbed his eyes and yawned. "Don't know. I'd hire you here, but—what with the big fees I'll be earning on the United Financial case—it wouldn't look good. Might seem like I put you up to something."

Staring out the window again, Wayne sighed. "I suppose you're right."

"Buck up, my friend," Grisham said encouragingly. "You should be proud of what you've done. And it's not the end of the world. Maybe Thelma can support you two for awhile. I hear she talked some rich collector into buying that godawful piece of junk art she did—the Freedom Rider made out of wire hangers—for five grand."

Wayne smiled weakly. "Yeah. Pretty amazing, isn't it?"

Grisham shrugged. "Just goes to show you," he said, absently reaching for the phone to place another call. "Some folks will believe anything you tell 'em. Anything!"

A PLACE APART

By all accounts, Marty Regal emerged from Betty Ford a changed man. Rehab, it seemed, had brought about a spiritual awakening in the young investment banker. Twenty-eight days of Morning Reflections, Meditation Walks, Group Therapy, Step Studies, Personal Counseling and Patient Education (not to mention high-fat, high-cholesterol meals) had apparently converted the cynical, hard-boiled financial deal-maker into a selfless do-gooder determined to make the world a better place.

"You know, I've been thinking . . . ." Marty said to Tom Mullins, his twelve-step "sponsor," over lunch at Schrafft's.

"Hold it right there," barked Mullins, a burly Wall Street back office veteran and AA old-timer. "A guy only forty-two days sober's got no business thinking. You should be following direction. You know what they say—'My best thinking got me here.'"

"Yes, but . . . ."

"And no 'yes, butting' out of you, either, my friend. It's a sure sign of denial."

Marty stabbed his fork into his fruit salad in frustration. It was still difficult for the highly-paid Prudent Securities VP to be lectured like a small child, particularly by a low-level employee of a competitor firm.

"Okay, okay. No more thinking, no more 'yes, butting'— I promise. It's just that I was wondering how many people there are on Wall Street like me—you know, investment bankers who are alcoholics and addicts—who aren't in a recovery program because they feel there's no one to turn to, no place to go."

"AA's in the phone book," Mullins replied curtly, slicing ferociously into an extra-rare Porterhouse steak. "All you've got to do is call and they'll be happy to direct you to any one of the over 3,000 meetings in the New York metropolitan area. It's not rocket science, you know. Even someone as screwed up as you can do it!"

Marty stared blankly at his sponsor, astonished at his apparent insensitivity. Talking to Mullins was like having a conversation with a recorded message.

"That's easy for you to say, Tom. You know all about AA. But I'm sure there are many financial professionals out there—particularly those, like me, with blue-chip firms—who feel they wouldn't be welcome in a twelve-step program. They may be wrong, but that's how they feel."

Mullins grimaced, as if he had just swallowed a raw egg. Although a man accustomed to listening to the babbling of "newcomers," he'd never ceased to be amazed by what he considered the mindless drivel of which they were capable.

"Jesus Christ, you rehab types are all alike," he chided his AA charge in a voice that could be heard several tables away. "Always talking about feelings. Hell, if I acted on my feelings all the time, I'd be slumped against a dumpster right now, sucking down a bottle of T-Bird wrapped in a paper bag."

With that, Mullins grabbed a large bottle of mineral water, hoisted it to his mouth and took a long swig. "Ahh!" he belched. "And, as far as being a 'blue-chip' professional is concerned, you didn't look so blue-chip when I fished you out of the drunk tank a couple of months ago, with all those cuts and bruises on your face. In fact, you looked like you'd *bottomed out!*"

Marty could see that he was getting nowhere, but, if nothing else, his penchant for negotiation had survived his rehabilitation.

"All I'm saying is that it might be a good idea if someone started a meeting specifically for investment bankers. It might make them more comfortable if they knew they were fighting the battle against chemical dependency alongside their peers. I mean, even now, there are lawyer groups, accountant groups, doctor groups, gay and lesbian groups, atheist groups, groups for clergymen . . . . "

"And every damn one of them is a lousy idea — a product of Stinkin' Thinkin'. Listen, kid, if there's one thing you learn in AA, it's humility — that's what anonymity is all about. Chemical dependency? In my book, a friggin' drunk is a friggin' drunk."

"Well," answered Marty, "it was just an idea."

"Son, just climb down from that pink cloud of yours and take the advice of someone who knows. Quit wasting your time with pie-in-the-sky theories and just stick to the basics of staying sober — like doing your Fourth Step — your moral inventory? I'm sure you've got enough character defects to write about to make a best-seller. As they say, 'First Things First.'"

Marty didn't act on his idea for several months. By then, drowning in AA shibboleths, smothered by program pieties and convinced that the cliché-ridden Tom Mullins was an "AA Nazi," he had dismissed his cantankerous sponsor and replaced him with Jay Thompson, a considerably more flexible tutor in sobriety.

Marty had met Jay — a mergers and acquisitions specialist at Drexel, Birnbaum & Co. — at a regular noontime AA meeting held in the basement of the American Stock Exchange. They hit it off immediately. For one thing, the two young investment bankers looked remarkably alike —

from their boyish faces and wavy blond hair to their tailored pin-stripped suits, matching suspenders and solid color shirts and ties. Jay's story was almost identical to Marty's. A Harvard MBA with a taste for vodka and cocaine, Jay had succeeded on Wall Street through a combination of innate ability, intestinal fortitude, hard work and guile. In the months before he got sober, Jay told Marty, he'd found himself relying more and more on the latter quality to get by. Unfortunately, he didn't fool those closest to him, including his wife, who'd left him with their two young daughters in tow.

Jay — thirteen months sober when he and Marty first met — immediately embraced Marty's enthusiasm for establishing a fellowship of recovering investment bankers. He saw more in it than simply the opportunity to be of service to others.

"Think of the possibilities for networking," he told Marty late one afternoon as they sat at the bar in Harry's at Hanover Square, munching on trail mix and sipping Perrier, exchanging the latest financial scuttlebutt. "Just look around this place, for instance. I bet one out of every three guys in here is a drunk. Yet this crowd includes some of the most talented, well-connected and well-paid professionals in the country. Getting them to share what they know once a week could be a real bonanza for guys like us."

Marty shifted uncomfortably on his stool. As much as he'd detested Tom Mullins's relentless sloganeering, he'd taken at least some of his former mentor's gospel to heart. And one principle that had been drilled into him was that the purpose of AA was to carry the message of sobriety — not to provide an opportunity to meet prospects and cut business deals.

"Of course, Jay, the networking aspect would be secondary, incidental. Sobriety would come first. Right?"

The merger and acquisitions specialist smiled reassuringly. "Of course. Besides, by having our own AA meeting, we can avoid running into clients. Good for anonymity — am I right, or what?"

"I guess . . . ."

Jay made arrangements for the necessary meeting space and a listing in the AA Directory. Marty prepared a flyer and had it posted in the windows of various downtown watering holes and on the bulletin boards of the major

A PLACE APART A Safe Haven for Wall Streeters Suffering From Alcoholism and Drug Addiction Thursdays at Noon Community Meeting Room 1 44 Pine Street Closed Meeting — Investment Bankers Only

lunch clubs in the Financial District.

Bankers in Alcoholics Anonymous (BAA) debuted on a brilliant spring day in Lower Manhattan. Unfortunately, attendance at the kickoff meeting approximated what might be expected at a seventy-fifth high school reunion. In addition to the two founders, only four curious souls appeared to launch the new organization, one of whom left early when he realized, halfway through the meeting, that A Place Apart was not the regular Thursday gathering of the Downtown Hispanic Lawyers Association (which convened two doors down). Nevertheless, the meeting went forward, with Jay unanimously elected as Secretary and Marty as Treasurer.

BAA suffered through weeks of lackluster attendance. To Marty, the poor turnout reflected the reluctance of the chemically-dependent to come to terms with their disease. Jay agreed, although with his usual twist.

"You know, Marty, we're pretty poor excuses for investment bankers," he declared after one sparsely-attended session. "Here we are in our second month of operation, and we don't even have a marketing plan!"

"A marketing plan?"

Jay put his arm around Marty's shoulders like a wise older brother. "Kid, selling sobriety is no different than pedaling stocks and bonds. You've got to promote, promote, promote. We can't just sit around waiting for the drunks to come to us. We've got to reach out and pull them in."

The uncomfortable feeling he'd experienced when first discussing A Place Apart with Jay returned to Marty. "That sounds fine, Jay," he conceded, fumbling through his dog-eared copy of *Twelve Steps and Twelve Traditions*. "But isn't there some AA principle that says that we're a program of attraction and not of promotion?"

"Buddy," Jay replied, "that's outmoded thinking. It might have worked in the Thirties, when the founders of AA were calling the shots, but it won't do in the Information Age. We need to market!"

Trusting in his sponsor—after all, Jay had more time in the program than he did—Marty reluctantly went along. Using his not inconsiderable personal funds, and calling in some personal favors, Jay orchestrated a media campaign worthy of a block-buster motion picture. First, he arranged to publish Marty's meeting notice in *The Wall Street Journal*, placing it prominently, for five consecutive days, among the "tombstone" ads for big financing and merger deals ("the tombstones," he declared, "are the first thing a good investment banker—even one with a nasty hangover— reads in the morning to get a jump on the market"). Next, he put up a BAA website on the Internet (www.whiteshoealcoholics.com), convincing AOL to include, for a small fee, a pop-up ad on its financial channel permitting users to click either "No Thanks" or "Tell Me More" on their screens. Finally, he hired a telemarketing firm to call supervisory personnel at big brokerage houses to suggest that, if they were aware of employees having drug or alcohol problems, they intervene and direct them to A Place Apart.

While impressed with Jay's efforts on behalf of BAA, Marty feared that perhaps his sponsor was going a bit overboard.

"Don't worry," Jay assured him. "I just want to be of service. You could say I'm making an investment in the future. Anyway, isn't financial largesse called for by AA's Sixth Tradition—or is it the Seventh?"

"Something like that," Marty replied uneasily.

Jay's PR blitz seemed to work. The promotional campaign attracted ever-increasing numbers to the weekly meeting. At first, most were experienced AA hands—older investment bankers, with years of sobriety, curious about the fledgling organization. They—perhaps uncomfortable attending a meeting run by two neophytes—did not return for a second visit. Eventually, however, more and more young men and women—many of whom had never attended an AA meeting before—joined the group as newcomers. The fresh arrivals included many up-and-coming Wall Street stars familiar to Marty and Jay.

"I can't believe that Susan Watkins is one of us," Jay marvelled after one meeting attended by over thirty new arrivals. "*Fortune* listed her as one of the top twenty women under forty on Wall Street. Who would have thought she was an addict? What a fraud she is! And Tim Lyons—that guy is such a royal pain in the ass in merger negotiations. I only wish I'd known before that he was a common drunk! That information sure would have come in handy when he had me over a barrel at the conference table."

BAA suffered the normal growing pains of any new AA organization—newcomers forgetting (or refusing) to identify themselves as "alcoholics" or "addicts," backsliders ducking out of meetings to imbibe from pint bottles or take quick hits in the washrooms, tipsy members accepting thirty-day chips, constant grousing about the decaffeinated coffee, the poor sound system and the restrictive meeting rules (over Jay's objections, cell phones and beepers were banned by a "group conscience"), trash left around chairs and tables, and so forth. A Place Apart also experienced problems unique to a haven for investment bankers. These included complaints about the presence of research analysts, considered by many to be a breach of the sacred "Chinese Wall" principles of Wall Street (to allay fears, Marty assured the group that "what you say here stays here"); a move to bar attendance at the meeting by commercial bankers (presumably a violation, at least in spirit, of the long-established separation of the commercial banking and investment banking businesses on the Street); suggestions that the meeting time be changed to five o'clock, after regular trading hours; and a controversy over the bona fides of certain "consultants" and "finders" who held themselves out to be investment bankers but whose credentials as such were questionable.

Jay reacted to complaints by cavalierly suggesting that the malcontents simply leave and go elsewhere (which many did). Nevertheless, the meeting continued to thrive, eventually developing a hard core of adherents, most of whom had less than a month of sobriety when they first arrived.

42

Following a "general participation" format, each gathering saw one troubled investment banker after another—many resembling melancholy automatons—come to the podium to share about their personal problems—the alienation of family, friends and colleagues, the loss of self-confidence and self-esteem, the shame of repeated "slips" and the emptiness of life without alcohol or drugs. Often, tears would well in Marty's eyes as he listened; he could personally identify with every one of them.

Jay, less sympathetic, remained dry-eyed. He sometimes expressed irritation when a member launched into a soliloquy about personal difficulties, frequently, in his capacity as secretary, cutting them off with something like "Please wrap it up, Dolores—you're not pitching a client, after all." And he never once shared himself. Rather, Jay seemed most enthusiastic about the informal socializing that occurred after each meeting. Featuring not only traditional AA hugs, kisses and handshakes, "Fellowship Time" (as Jay styled it) also involved the exchange of business cards, small talk about developments in the professional world and conversations about pending deals.

One day Jay made an unexpected announcement. Dispensing with the traditional reading from Chapter Five of the AA "Big Book," he described "a modest change in format" he intended to implement in his capacity as Secretary.

"I think we would all agree," he said, a look of earnestness and sincerity on his face, "that the general participation format has been of some value. However, I believe that we are not taking full advantage of the fact that this is a meeting of investment bankers. The very purpose of this meeting—which Marty and I decided early on to call 'A Place Apart'—is to emphasize our uniqueness as alcoholics and addicts who work on Wall Street. If we only hear about common, everyday problems like an unhappy spouse or an angry boss, a prolonged depression or a relapse, we might as well be going to another meeting—one on Skid Row populated by streetwalkers, derelicts and other undesirables."

An eery silence gripped the audience as Jay, taking a swig of diet soda and clearing his throat, continued.

"No, my friends, we deserve better—something more relevant to all our lives. Accordingly, as your secretary, I am instituting a new policy. Starting today, all sharing must focus on the problems you face as investment bankers in sobriety. I want to hear specifics about the stress of the big deals you're working on, the mistakes you've made advising clients, the guilt you've experienced hard-selling your services, even the crimes you've committed against investors. No more of this 'sharing in a general way.' I want to see genuine honesty in this room! Those who stray from the new format will be asked to leave. They don't belong here!"

Marty was stunned. Not only had Jay failed to consult him about the new directive, but what Jay called "targeted sharing" seemed half-baked and dangerous. When one member meekly suggested the taking of another "group conscience," Jay ruled him out-of-order.

After the meeting, Marty confronted his sponsor in the lobby.

"Jay, have you been smoking dope? That format change . . . is . . . well . . . a questionable idea. First of all, BAA is supposed to be a bridge to Alcoholics Anonymous, not a barrier. We shouldn't encourage our members to think they're different from other alcoholics and addicts. Plus, it's an AA tradition to share in a general way. Asking people to get specific discourages openness. And what if there's a breach of confidentiality . . . ?"

"Oh, just relax, will you, Marty?" Jay interrupted, popping two red pills into his mouth. "You're exaggerating. First, investment bankers are different. Anyone worth his salt eats, drinks, sleeps and dreams his work — it's an obsession. If we don't make these guys talk about their careers — and be specific — we'll be encouraging dishonesty. And that's contrary to the fundamental principles of the program.

"As for the chilling effect, you have nothing to worry about. Christ, most of these people are total novices — they're lonely, frightened, unsure of themselves. Because of that, they're more amenable to following direction. They'll be like putty in our hands; they'll listen to old-timers like you and me.

"And, as for confidentiality, you said it yourself — 'what you say here stays here.'"

"Yes, but . . . ."

"Marty, as your sponsor, I admonish you not to 'yes, but' me. Just get with the program."

Marty soon began missing meetings of A Place Apart. At first, he found himself tied up on a multitude of new deals that seemed to require round-the-clock attention (since getting sober, Prudent Securities had made him Deputy Coordinator of its EPG (Esoteric Products Group)). Then he undertook a reconciliation with his wife, Eileen. Reunited after a one-year separation, the two went off on a ten-day Caribbean cruise. When he returned, he was informed that he'd been elected a Managing Director of the Wall Street powerhouse. Even when things slowed down a bit, there always seemed to be better things to do at noon than go to an AA meeting — have lunch with a client, shoot the breeze in the firm cafeteria, place a call to a prospect or read the latest financial news on the Internet.

Eventually, his conscience started to bother him. He felt guilty about missing so many meetings: he wondered how the newcomers were doing; he was concerned that they might think he'd abandoned them; he even worried about whether his prolonged absence would undermine his own AA program. Then, one Thursday, he suddenly realized that a year had passed since he'd gotten sober. Because the celebration of "anniversaries" was part of the meeting's format, he decided to attend that day's session.

Marty was appalled when he arrived in Community Meeting Room 1. Rather than the crowd of hopeful AAers he was used to seeing, there were only a handful of woeful-looking young people milling about aimlessly, like commuters stranded at the wrong station stop. The folding chairs, normally set out in neat rows in front of the podium, were stacked in piles on the floor. The coffee maker, around which many members gathered prior to the meeting, lay in a box in a closet, along with the inspirational posters customarily hanging on the walls and the books and pamphlets usually stacked on a table in the back. A young woman was rummaging around, apparently trying to find the format for the meeting. Marty felt as if he had walked into an abandoned land sales office.

"What happened?" he asked.

"Simple," someone volunteered. "People are leaving the meeting like rats fleeing a fire. The guy with the set-up commitment—Joe W.—relapsed after he told the group how he had cheated on expense vouchers. Linda P.—the coffee person—walked out of the last meeting when she shared about having an affair with a partner at her firm, and Jay insisted that she name names. The literature guy just stopped coming. I guess he thought we were making a mockery of the Twelve Steps."

Marty shook his head in disbelief. "But where is Jay?" he asked. Shoulders shrugged in unison.

Despite the chaos, Marty decided to go on with the meeting, volunteering to serve as temporary secretary. After everyone pulled up a chair, and someone read from Chapter Five, Marty opened the meeting up to participation. A swarm of hands shot up.

"I'm Steve K., alcoholic and addict. And I just want to say that I think the confidentiality of this meeting has been compromised. Two weeks ago I stood up here and shared about how stressed out I was about a presentation I had to make to a new client — that I wasn't sure my firm could really handle the work. Then, yesterday I find out that other bankers came in and stole the business right out from under us. They told the client that we weren't up to the task! If my bosses ever find out what I did, I'll be fired!"

"Yeah, the same thing happened to me," a woman in the back piped up. "I'm Katherine L., alcoholic. I talked here about a friendly merger a client was negotiating — about how my twenty-hour workdays kept me from meetings and threatened my sobriety. Well, the next morning I read in the *Times* that somebody else has launched a hostile bid for the same company — using another banking firm."

"What about me?" chimed in a pock-marked young man jumping to his feet? "My firm came up with a new product idea that I was worried wouldn't pass IRS muster. This morning the Treasury Department put out a ruling that our idea didn't work. They said they'd been tipped off by a competitor firm. Jesus, our clients have already done over a billion dollars of deals! We could be ruined!"

Marty's stomach churned as he listened. Although he really didn't have to, he nevertheless asked the three what investment banking firm was involved.

"Drexel, Birnbaum," came the answer.

Sensing that further sharing might provoke violence — or perhaps worse, a collective relapse — Marty suggested that the meeting be adjourned to the following Thursday and that, in the interim, everyone call his or her sponsor, and attend at least two AA meetings, daily.

The unhappy bankers all rose, formed a crude circle, joined hands and began to recite the Serenity Prayer:

"God, Grant Me the Serenity to Accept the Things I Cannot Change, the Courage to Change the Things I Can, and the Wisdom . . . ."

Just then, a commotion arose in the hallway outside. Suddenly, the doors burst open and a horde of men rushed in like stampeding buffalo, then fanned out across the room. Several, their coats flung open, displayed pistols in shoulder holsters; others flashed badges. Heading the charge was a heavy-set, middle-age man with tousled hair, dressed in a threadbare gray suit, waving a pair of handcuffs over his head.

"Okay, which one of you is Darren Driver?" he demanded. "I have a warrant for your arrest — on charges of insider trading and mail fraud. Give up, Driver, and make things easy for yourself."

Marty immediately recognized the leader of the invading phalanx of government agents as Mitchell A. Palmer, Deputy State's Attorney for White Collar and Victimless Crime, a career prosecutor with a penchant for getting his name and face in the papers by leading a one-man crusade against financial wrongdoing on Wall Street.

Marty also recognized the name of Darren Driver. As Darren D., he'd often come to A Place Apart, always raising his hand when Jay asked newcomers in their first thirty days of sobriety to identify themselves. Driver — a Reed, Morgan & Sons mergers specialist — was generally regarded as Jay's principal competitor on the Street.

48

When Palmer was satisfied that Driver was not present, he announced that everyone was free to go. "But you'll be hearing from me soon," he warned ominously as the discouraged AAers shuffled out of the room like bombed-out refugees. "I have a few questions I want to ask."

~ ~

Marty was not overly-concerned with the grand jury subpoena served upon him the next day. It sought testimony about any revelations of criminal activities that may have occurred at meetings of A Place Apart. Since he hadn't attended any meetings during the weeks immediately following the "change in format," he had nothing to testify to. The newcomers who had sought refuge there, however, would not be so fortunate.

Jay never returned any of Marty's phone messages. He always seemed to be out-of-town, in a meeting or otherwise "tied up" when Marty called. In spite of Mitchell Palmer's investigation, which served only to embarrass those who had shared their feelings at A Place Apart, Jay continued to make a name for himself at Drexel, Birnbaum. In fact, he was named "Deal-Maker of the Year" by the *Journal*, primarily in recognition of his work in helping to bring about a major consolidation in the pharmaceutical industry.

Marty eventually asked Tom Mullins to be his sponsor again. After delivering a half-hour tongue-lashing to his errant former disciple in his office, Mullins accepted.

"Now, my friend, it's back to 'First Things First.' I want you to begin your Fourth Step list of character defects immediately. Start with your resentments . . . ."

"No, no, Tom," Marty interrupted. "With all due respect, I think I should start off with my principal character defect."

"What's that?" asked Mullins.

Marty smiled knowingly. "Do you really have to ask?" the born-again skeptic answered.

CELEBRITY

Barton Grand always traveled first class. The sandy-haired investment banker—selected as one of the "Top 20 Under 40" in the July 1995 issue of *American Finance* magazine—had grown accustomed to five-star hotels, gourmet restaurants, stretch limos and fawning subordinates. He deserved first-cabin treatment, he thought to himself, as he took off his suit jacket, loosened his blue and white striped tie, adjusted his red suspenders and settled into his recliner seat on the early morning flight to LA.

Lying back and closing his eyes, Barton smiled contentedly while less fortunate passengers—suitcases, garment bags and screaming youngsters in tow, grim and anxious expressions on their faces—trooped past him like displaced persons on the march to a refugee camp.

Just as the "Fasten Seat Belt" sign began flashing overhead, a flight attendant in a blue jacket came up the aisle and tapped Barton on the shoulder.

"Sorry to bother you, sir . . . ."

"I'll have a glass of orange juice," the startled young businessman said reflexively. "No, make that a mimosa!"

"Please, sir," the attendant continued, "may I see your boarding pass?"

The steward took the ticket stub and peered at it like a cop examining the license and registration of a driver pulled over for speeding. "I think we have a problem," he said stiffly. "I'll be right back."

A sudden commotion arose in the front of the cabin. Barton looked up to see four disheveled young men in dark glasses, dragging what appeared to be musical instrument cases, standing in the doorway. Clad in scruffy jeans and dungarees, they wore identical T-shirts, an expletive emblazoned across the front. They were accompanied by a young woman with stringy blond hair, wearing a granny dress, a large floppy hat and sandals. One of the young intruders was scribbling something on the back of an emergency instruction card for an excited stewardess.

The steward hurriedly consulted the flight service director and then returned.

"I apologize, sir, but it seems we're over-booked in first class. I'm afraid we'll have to move you to the . . . er . . . main cabin. Of course, you'll be entitled to an appropriate refund . . . ."

Barton gazed at the ragged troupe in disbelief. "You mean you're bumping me for that collection of losers?" he bellowed.

The steward turned red. "You could look at it that way. But, actually, that 'collection of losers' is Metal Mayhem — the rock band. Unfortunately, they've brought a groupie along — the blonde — without telling us in advance. That often happens on this flight. But it's our policy to accommodate celebrities. And, in any event, we're not really 'bumping' you, sir, only asking you to move back. I'm sure you understand."

Barton was indignant. How could they ask him — the top graduate of the Drexel Business School Class of 1990 — to give up his seat for a rock band that no one would remember a year from now? Barton Grand — the inventor of such corporate merger strategies as the "Upside/Down Option," "The Flaming Phoenix Defense" and the "Golden Noose?" It was like bumping Thomas Aquinas for Billy Sunday. (Barton silently congratulated himself on this analogy.)

52

"Look, buddy," he roared at the attendant, "I'm an important guy too, you know."

"Of course you are, sir," the attendant replied condescendingly, as if addressing an unruly child. "All of our passengers are important to us."

"No, no, you don't understand. I was voted Young Dealmaker of the Year for 1996 by the Downtown Business Council. In fact, there's an article in your passenger service magazine that mentions my name."

Barton rummaged through the seat-back pocket in front of him. Finding the glossy in-flight magazine, he quickly flipped through the sticky pages. Unable to find what he was looking for, he grabbed the copy from the seat next to him and awkwardly fumbled through it.

"I don't understand," he complained. "It was on page 123 . . . ."

The steward bent over and stared at the page Barton held up to his face. "That's the crossword puzzle, sir," he said with a sly smile. "Perhaps you were thinking of last month's issue. We just replaced the magazine this morning. We don't like to bother our passengers with . . . er . . . yesterday's news."

Just then, a grainy female voice came over the public address system. "Flight 123 is preparing for immediate departure. All passengers should now be in their seats, with their seat-backs upright and their seatbelts securely fastened."

The flight service director, a stocky man carrying a walkie-talkie, approached the steward and whispered something in his ear. He then turned to Barton.

"Sir, we do have first class space available on our next flight out to the Coast—in three hours. I can, if you wish, book you on that . . . ."

"I can't wait three hours! I've got a meeting with an unhappy client who's threatening to fire . . . ." He hesitated. "I've got to be in LA this afternoon—and that's all there is to it!"

"Well, then, you'll either have to move back or get off the plane and find another airline to take you there. Under the law, I have full authority . . . ."

"Okay, okay," Barton replied, throwing up his hands in resignation. "But your CEO will be hearing from me! I have a lot of influence in high places, you know!"

As the steward rolled his eyes, Barton rose to his feet and watched the usurpers scramble into their seats like boisterous youngsters getting onto a carnival ride.

"Hey, bro."

"Thanks, dude."

"Right on."

As he walked away, his jacket slung over his shoulder, clutching his briefcase, Barton glared haughtily at the celebrities. One of them flashed a peace sign.

Once settled in the nearly-empty coach cabin, Barton smiled faintly. Oh well, he thought, at least this should make interesting cocktail party conversation: banished to steerage by a rock group—-fifteen-minute celebrities. Might make a good story for his next interview in the financial press—an innocent victim of distorted social priorities—a martyr to misguided cultural values. Someone might be interested. Maybe.

A DEATH IN THE FAMILY

Sudden death can strike a devastating blow to any family. The family of Allen & White, attorneys-at-law, is no exception.

And so it was that, on a brilliant spring day in 1996, when Harry Compton made the fateful decision to cross 50th Street at Lexington against the light, oblivious to the Browning-Ferris behemoth barreling toward the intersection, the anguish and grief of his untimely passing reached into every corner of the white shoe law firm.

"Poor Mr. Compton," sobbed Molly Sparrow, Director of Telephonic Services and thirty-year veteran of the Allen & White switchboard. "He was such a dedicated young lawyer. They say he was rushing to a meeting with a client when it happened."

"Tough break," noted C. Michael Manley, head of the Corporate Department. "Harry was a shoo-in for partner. But at least he died with his boots on."

"A tragedy for us all," wrote J. Thornton Hightower, Senior Partner and leader of the Bar, in an e-mail message marked "Personal" addressed to "All Users Worldwide." "Harry's death reminds us of the thin thread by which we all cling to this life. There will never be another like him."

But, privately, Hightower had a somewhat different spin on the tragedy. "Associates are, by nature, impermanent," he assured Harry's clients over the phone, reading from a note card. "[Fill in Blank] has already taken over all Harry's work for you. It's like nothing ever happened."

Whatever his true thoughts, it fell to the Senior Partner to notify Harry's next of kin that the esteemed young associate had been struck down on the streets of

Manhattan, ending up, in the words of one of the City's Finest, "looking like a pumpkin tossed from the top of Citicorp Center." When Harry's personnel records revealed his only surviving relative to be a ninety-five-year-old great aunt confined to an upstate nursing home, Hightower decided to fulfill his Senior Partnerly duties by sending his condolences to her via a fax stamped "PLEASE DELIVER ASAP" and bearing the legend: "THIS DOCUMENT IS SENT BY A LAW FIRM AND CONTAINS INFORMATION THAT MAY BE PRIVILEGED AND CONFIDENTIAL. IF YOU ARE NOT THE INTENDED RECIPIENT, PLEASE DESTROY AND NOTIFY US IMMEDIATELY." Not surprisingly, the message was lost on the intended recipient.

After a search of the records of the firm's Trusts and Estates Department indicated that Harry Compton had died intestate, Hightower ordered the associate's remains turned over to a funeral home for cremation and his ashes scattered in Battery Park, at a cost of $1,000. This amount was deducted from Harry's final paycheck, along with several taxicab fares the young lawyer had failed to charge to client accounts prior to his passing.

A simple memorial service was held the following week. (Under the firm's policy regarding associate perks, lawyers having four or more years of continuous service were entitled to a farewell lunch at the time of their departure, or, if departure were due to death, a memorial service.) Attended by eleven lawyers and staff members, the gathering convened at four o'clock in the Community Meeting Room in the basement of the firm's downtown headquarters, a facility normally reserved for convocations of Twelve-Step groups and political activists.

(Arrangements to broadcast the event live to firm personnel worldwide were cancelled when no lawyer at any of Allen & White's fifteen branch offices expressed an interest in participating.)

Standing behind a podium at the front of the musty meeting room, against a backdrop of wall posters proclaiming "One Day at a Time," "Serenity Now," "Viva Cesar Chavez" and "Malcolm Lives," the white-haired Senior Partner waxed eloquent on the many contributions of Harry Compton to the practice of Allen & White.

"Harry was a lawyer's lawyer," Hightower observed to the stone-faced assembly, "a professional among professionals. Conscientious, hard-working, always willing to pitch in, there was no task he couldn't perform, no deal he couldn't close, no legal problem he couldn't overcome. He never let us down."

Yielding the podium, Hightower asked for reminiscences from the audience. A teary-eyed Quentin Matthews, Vice Chairman of the firm, related how Harry had once billed a client twenty-seven hours for a single day's work by flying from New York to Los Angeles in the morning, spending the afternoon and early evening proofreading a stock prospectus at the printer, and returning on the red-eye flight late that night. A reflective Sidney Wrangler, chief of the firm's Mergers and Acquisitions Group, told of how, during one heated takeover battle, Harry had learned the secret plans of the opposition by impersonating a Federal Securities Bureau staffer over the phone ("The guy made Rich Little look like a novice"). C. Michael Manley fondly recalled how Harry had closed three different deals on the morning of a power failure in the Financial District while, at the same time, hosting an international conference call on a global bond offering.

"But enough of these office war stories," interjected the Senior Partner. "We all know about Harry's legal prowess.

Let's hear a few personal reminiscences. Do I have any volunteers?"

The sparsely-populated audience reacted as if Hightower had asked for a show of hands on how many regularly cheated on expense vouchers or pilfered office supplies. Silence filled the room, as those in attendance exchanged nervous and embarrassed glances. No one came forward.

"Oh, come now," the Senior Partner prodded, "surely one of you can tell us something of his life away from the office—of his outside interests, his favorite activities, his hopes, his dreams . . . . "

The mourners, apparently stumped, remained blank-faced and silent. Glancing at his watch, Hightower decided he could still catch the five-fifteen to New Canaan. Thanking the participants, he declared the memorial service to be at an end.

～　～

The next day, J. Thornton Hightower ordered a full-scale investigation into the personal life of the late Harry Compton.

"I just don't understand it," the baffled Senior Partner told Hank Persons, the firm's Director of Security. "Here's a young associate who everybody thought the world of. He had the reputation of being one of the most knowledgeable and competent lawyers at the firm. He could do anything and everything. He was a respected member of the Allen & White family. Yet, apparently, nobody knows anything about him."

"Maybe he had something to hide," suggested the balding, bloated former PI.

"You may be right. For all we know, this Compton fellow could have spent his off-duty hours dealing drugs in Central Park, manufacturing plastic explosives in his apartment or parading about Greenwich Village at night in a blond wig, a skin-tight dress and high heels, soliciting perverted sex. We could be embarrassed or, even worse, blackmailed if something negative comes out. We have to find out who this guy was!"

The Director of Security had little to go on. According to witnesses at the scene, in the moments before the police arrived, a group of homeless men had relieved Harry's battered corpse of everything in his possession—his watch, his wallet, his briefcase, his key chain, a pair of plastic sunglasses, even a removable porcelain tooth. Harry's office likewise yielded no clues as to his true identity. Apart from the disorderly stacks of papers, law books, mementos and pencils, pens and other assorted materials and supplies typical of an overworked associate's office, the only item of interest was an empty spray can labeled "Bullshit Repellent," apparently given to him by someone as a joke.

Under intense grilling by Persons, Harry's secretary reported that, at the office, he never entertained personal visitors, never received personal phone calls, never got personal mail and maintained no personal files. Employee records listed no physician, dentist, optometrist, clergyman, club membership or outside activity. As "Person to Contact in Case of Emergency," Harry had put down Molly Sparrow. The Harvard Law School Alumni Office, once satisfied that Harry was actually dead and had left no will (and therefore nothing to his alma mater), reported having had no contact with the Order of the Coif graduate and *Law Review* editor since his departure from the school's ivied confines. Scores of associates confirmed that they had never been to his apartment, had him over for dinner, accompanied him to a movie or ball game, or just hung out with Harry outside of work. A number of the associates, in fact, told Persons that they thought Harry never left the office except on business. Apparently, the workaholic attorney was never "off duty."

Stymied by standard investigative techniques, Persons resorted to breaking and entering. Having no keys to Harry's Westside walk-up, and unable to locate the super, he decided to rely on self-help. Armed with only a screwdriver and nail file, the diligent sleuth succeeded in gaining access to Harry's personal sanctuary. There, he found no drugs or drug paraphernalia, no dynamite or explosive caps, no wigs, dresses or high heels. What he did find he described in an "EYES ONLY" memo he penned the next day to Thornton Hightower. The following is an excerpt from that memo:

"As best I can tell, Harry Compton had no life outside the office. He lived alone in a run-down studio apartment with a family of cockroaches and other assorted vermin. He had no television, VCR, CD or tape player, or personal computer—only a small clock radio he kept on a night stand next to his bed. He had only one extra suit, one extra pair of dress shoes, three extra ties and an assortment of ragged underwear, socks and shirts. The only books I found in his apartment were *Income Taxes for Dummies (1990 Edition)* and *1001 Jokes About Lawyers*. Other items of note were:

1. Notices of Discontinuance of Service from Consolidated Edison and New York Telephone (dated two weeks prior to his death).

2. A partially-completed Form 1040 for the year 1994.

3. A three-month-old, unopened letter, marked "URGENT," from the Student Loan Assistance Corporation.

4. An imitation Tiffany clock not yet set for Daylight Saving Time.

5. A Chase Manhattan checking account statement showing a balance on deposit of $270,581.83.

"Upon completing my investigation, two words came to mind: LOSER and DEADBEAT. This guy clearly was not Supreme Court material!"

Hightower was relieved that (but for the unfiled tax return and dunning notices) Persons's investigation had revealed no serious skeletons in Harry Compton's closet.

"But, when you think about it," he confided to Quentin Matthews, "we really dodged a bullet. Imagine, we were less than a year away from making that joker a partner!"

Satisfied that there was nothing more to learn about Harry Compton, the Senior Partner dispatched his files on the deceased attorney to a paralegal in the Trusts and Estates Group, with the instructions "Pls. handle and dispose of."

But Hightower remained perplexed. "I don't understand," he said, shaking his head, as he handed the thin manila file folder on Harry Compton to his secretary. "He was a member of the family. I just don't understand."

THE WIZARD OF WALL STREET
(A Fable of Finance)

By Wall Street's exacting standards, Paul Gillespie was a mere journeyman. Although the boyish-looking broker consistently made money for his firm and its well-heeled clients, this was not, at the time, remarkable, for markets were rising. Modest success required of Paul only an uncritical acceptance of current thinking, served up daily in the tout sheets, over the squawk box and on CNBC. Of course, like most young investment professionals, Paul longed to one day distinguish himself from his peers. Unfortunately, no one had ever told him how.

Early one evening, as Paul sat at the bar in Harry's at Hanover Square—Wall Street's favorite after-market-hours hangout—he was approached by a stout, white-haired gentleman, dressed in a dark suit and clutching a dog-eared copy of *Fortune*. While dignified-looking, the man (like the magazine he carried) had clearly seen better days. "Excuse me, sir," he said, taking the stool next to Paul's. "Could you stand a fellow a drink?"

Normally, Paul brushed aside panhandlers with a sneer and a brusque remark. However, having made tidy gains for clients that day on a new stock issue, he felt in an unusually generous mood.

"Sure, old-timer. What'll you have?"

The man ordered a scotch, then quickly downed it. "Thank you, my friend," he said, getting up to leave. "I've always believed that one good deed deserves another. So take my advice: buy Amalgamated Steel common!"

63

With that, he walked away, disappearing into the throng of boisterous patrons.

Paul laughed off the advice: after all, Amalgamated Steel was on the firm's "sell" list. He forgot about the incident until, the following week, he came across an item in the back pages of the *Journal*: "Amalgamated Steel Announces Record Earnings; Beats Street Estimates by Wide Margin; Stock Soars on News."

No, it can't be, he said to himself. It was just a fluke.

Nevertheless, that evening, he sought out the old gentleman at Harry's. Fighting his way through the crowded, smoke-filled barroom, he found the stranger hovering over a recently-vacated table, sifting through newspapers, magazines and other odds and ends left behind by previous occupants.

"Hello, old-timer," he said. "What are you looking for?"

Startled, the man looked up and smiled mischievously. "Good information," he replied. "Can't do anything without good information."

"Do you remember me?" asked Paul, ignoring the man's odd behavior.

"Of course. You're the young fellow who was kind enough to buy me a drink last week. Tell me, did you follow my advice?"

Paul smiled stiffly. "To be honest, I didn't, and I'm kicking myself for it. Do you have another tip for me? I'll buy you another drink," he added, pointing in the direction of the bar.

Once again, the stranger, thanking Paul for his generosity, ordered a scotch, rapidly polished it off and stood up to leave. "Take my advice," he said. "Buy Consolidated Industries bonds."

Puzzled, Paul nevertheless thanked the man for the tip.

The next day, the youthful stockbroker bought the bonds for his clients. He hesitated at first, knowing that the company was bankrupt and that the bonds were valued by the market at only pennies on the dollar. But, because he was investing his clients' money, and not his own, he thought it worth the risk.

Soon, reports surfaced that a reorganization of Consolidated Industries was in the offing and that bondholders would be paid in full. Paul's clients made a killing.

This was no accident, Paul decided. The old man was a financial oracle—a stock market wizard.

Thereafter, Paul sought him out every evening after work. When not scouting out empty tables, he usually could be found sitting at the bar, reading a crumpled-up news article or financial report left by a departed patron. Paul would offer the stranger a drink and solicit a market tip. Worried that the old man could be breaching the confidences of others, Paul never asked his identity, or inquired as to the sources of his information. Nevertheless, the investments he recommended invariably proved highly profitable for Paul's clients, and earned substantial commissions for Paul and the firm.

Paul treated the stranger as something of a proprietary possession, like an antique clock or classic car locked away in storage; he never shared his advice with colleagues. Confident in his new source, Paul began to ignore the current wisdom of the firm and the marketplace on what to buy and what to sell, curtly dismissing it as "outmoded," "rubbish" and "drivel." Feeling entitled to share in his clients' good fortune, he put his own money into the market, at first in small amounts and only after investing his customers' funds, and then in ever larger amounts, before placing orders for clients. To his mind, he was doing nothing wrong: he was simply being rewarded for his generosity.

Paul flourished. Attracting press attention, he was called a "rising star" by one financial publication, a "stock market sorcerer" by another (compliments in which he wholeheartedly concurred). "We've entered a New Age," he said with an air of authority when asked his secret to successful investing. "A magical era of unlimited opportunity. Those who know the tricks will prosper."

The firm named Paul "Account Executive of the Year," promoting him to a senior position, with significant increases in pay and perks. One such perk was a month-long, all-expenses-paid vacation for two in the South Pacific. Tracking down an old college girlfriend, Paul, pitching himself as the successor to J.P. Morgan, convinced her to accompany him. Leaving his business affairs in the hands of harried colleagues, Paul departed, confident that nothing could go awry in a surging bull market.

Unfortunately, while he was away, the market lost its momentum, and eventually began to retreat: chip makers faltered, bio-techs stumbled and dot coms tumbled. Even the select investments of Paul and his clients were not immune to the down-draft. Losses abounded.

Panicking, Paul cut short his vacation and returned to New York. Desperate for advice on what to do next, he again sought out his mysterious mentor. The old gentleman, however, had disappeared.

"I told him to take a hike," the Harry's bartender informed the stunned stockbroker. "I didn't mind him at first. He seemed harmless enough, hanging around the bar, chatting up customers, bumming free drinks now and then. But, when the market turned south, he started getting on people's nerves: offering advice nobody wanted, getting into arguments. Some customers thought he was spying on them. So I gave him the old heave-ho."

Soon, government watchdogs (who, while times were good, had turned the other way) launched inquiries into the potentially fraudulent activities of those, like Paul, who'd in the past achieved sudden success in the market. The young broker, paralyzed with uncertainty, watched helplessly as his newly-acquired fortune evaporated, his reputation soured and his clients sold out and deserted him.

Then, one evening, he spotted the stranger outside the popular watering hole, bent over a dumpster, frantically rummaging through the garbage. His white hair was disheveled and dirty, his suit wrinkled and wet.

"Where have you been?" Paul barked, pulling the man away from the trash. "I've been looking for you everywhere."

The stranger seemed puzzled. "I've been around and about," he replied. "Here and there."

Paul grunted disagreeably. "Whatever," he said. "I need your advice. The market is collapsing. What should I do?"

The old gentleman scratched his head thoughtfully. "Take my advice," he said. "Buy low, sell high."

Paul's jaw dropped. "Buy low and sell high? What kind of advice is that? Everyone knows that old saw! Have you nothing better to offer?"

The stranger again scratched his head. "Uh . . . Take my advice . . . er . . . the trend is your friend . . . the best time to invest is now . . . wait for your window of opportunity . . . ."

Paul's face turned crimson. "Is that all I get, after the trust I've placed in you? Worn-out adages? Clichés? And gibberish, at that!"

The man shrugged. "What did you expect?" he asked. "A miracle?" With that, he returned his attention to the garbage.

Enraged at the flippant remark, Paul grabbed the man, lifted him up and threw him into the dumpster. Standing over him, he began pummeling him ferociously. There were shouts and screams nearby. Someone tackled Paul from behind and wrestled him to the pavement.

Paul learned the identity of his erstwhile benefactor in newspaper accounts of the incident the next day.

> "Police identified the victim as Clifford Willoughby, 75, formerly of Darien, Connecticut. Willoughby, once known as 'The Wizard of Wall Street' for his legendary investing prowess, gained notoriety nearly two decades ago when, after walking out on his lucrative stock brokerage business over what he derided as 'the herd mentality' of Wall Street, he mysteriously disappeared from public view. All but forgotten by the financial community, the eccentric investor apparently took to the streets of Lower Manhattan, living under various guises, giving out bits and pieces of quixotic advice to strangers, often in exchange for handouts and small favors. His motives in doing so remain unclear.

> "It is not known what relationship, if any, Willoughby had with his assailant."

Fortunately, the old man had suffered only minor cuts and bruises in the scuffle. Paul, however, was charged with assault. Still under investigation for stock fraud, he was placed on unpaid leave by his firm.

As a result of his misadventures, Paul, like all too many of his contemporaries on Wall Street, soon made the acquaintance of a lawyer. As he sat outside his new counsel's office, waiting for him to get off the phone, the journeyman stockbroker wondered if the attorney could perform a miracle where the stranger had failed. He doubted it.

THE EDUCATION OF STANLEY WHITEHEAD

Adventures of a White Shoe Lawyer

A MAN'S WORLD

Stanley Whitehead, his brow furrowed, sat in his corner office, sorting through the morning mail. Fumbling with the stack of correspondence overflowing his In Box, the crusty old attorney found it difficult to concentrate. Ever since arriving at the office that morning, he'd been brooding, like a monarch under siege pondering the imminent loss of an empire. The embattled Senior Partner had been weighing the alternatives: should he fight the forces of political correctness arrayed against him, risking a humiliating defeat, or simply abdicate, his dignity still intact?

Finally, in frustration, Stanley did what he always did when faced with a seemingly intractable problem: he buzzed his secretary on the intercom.

"Miss Jones, may I please have a word with you?"

The secretary, dressed in a brown tweed business suit, her silver hair done up in a bun, breezed into the office, pencil and notepad in hand. Seating herself in a sofa chair in front of her boss's enormous mahogany desk, she daintily crossed her legs, placed her notepad on her knees, flipped it open and prepared to take dictation.

"Miss Jones," the portly lawyer began, peering at his secretary over his half-moon glasses, "you know that staff training session we had yesterday—the one on ... er ... 'sensitivity in the workplace'?"

"Oh, yes, sir," she replied enthusiastically. "I found it most instructive."

Stanley, his mouth dry and pasty, coughed nervously. He tugged at his suspenders, fidgeted with his tie, scratched his mustache and ran his fingers through his bushy white hair. He scooped a letter opener off his desk, then banged it down like a gavel. He jumped, startled by the force of the blow.

"Sorry," he said sheepishly. "Now, Miss Jones, I want . . . uh . . . to make my own views on the matter . . . er . . . perfectly clear."

The secretary nodded. "Of course, Mr. Whitehead. You're the boss."

A faint smile crossed Stanley's face. He breathed easier.

"You see, Miss Jones," he continued, clearing his throat, "I arranged that session at the behest of the Management Committee. They've been after me for some time now to — as they put it — 'bring the firm out of the Dark Ages and into the Twenty-First Century.'"

"Oh, Mr. Whitehead," Miss Jones exclaimed. "The Dark Ages? Who would ever say a thing like that?"

"My sentiments exactly," Stanley replied. "But, getting back to my point, please understand that, while I don't necessarily disagree with many of the things that young female psychologist said yesterday, I hope that nothing she said — particularly about the proper relationship between a man . . . uh . . . I mean, a boss and his . . . er . . . a secretary — will interfere in any way with the special relationship you and I have shared these many years."

The secretary stared blankly at her employer, as if he'd just uttered something in tongues. "Of course," she answered hesitantly. "We've had a wonderful working relationship. At least, I think we have."

The Senior Partner beamed. "I'm glad to hear you say that, Miss Jones. I'm feeling better already."

Stanley stood up abruptly, then began pacing back and forth behind his desk. He rolled the letter opener in the palm of his hand like a knife thrower preparing to hurl his weapon at a volunteer from the audience. It dropped to the plushly-carpeted floor. Red-faced, he bent over and picked it up.

"Now, getting down to specifics," he said, pointing the dagger-like implement in the secretary's direction. "I'm sure you'll understand if, notwithstanding anything that young woman said about so-called interpersonal relations, I continue to refer to you as 'Miss Jones,' and ask that you continue to refer to me as 'Mr. Whitehead.' I admit it's a bit old-fashioned—perhaps even a tad stuffy—but that's just the way I am . . . . Old-fashioned, that is."

The secretary stirred uneasily. "I can see your point of view, Mr. Whitehead . . . ."

"And," he continued, his confidence growing, "you surely won't object if, say, I should hold a door open for you, or help you on with your coat, or let you get on an elevator ahead of me. It's what I was taught to do."

"Well, sir, I suppose chivalry isn't dead."

The Senior Partner, perceiving himself to be on a roll, reached into his shirt pocket and pulled out a thick brown cigar. He removed its plastic wrapper and punctured the tip, furtively eyeing his secretary for her reaction. "And, if you should catch me lighting up in my office—as I am about to do now—you won't hand me in to the smoking police, now will you?"

"Smoking police, sir? I didn't know we had smoking police . . . ."

"Excellent, excellent," he said, exhaling a foul-smelling cloud in the secretary's direction. "I think we see eye-to-eye."

"Of course, sir . . . ."

Stanley raised his hand to silence the secretary. "I don't want you getting the wrong impression, Miss Jones. You know I am the first to applaud the many advances achieved by the fair sex over the years. And I most certainly insist on strict adherence to our laws concerning discrimination and harassment. But, having said that, to someone of my generation, the business and professional realm remains fundamentally a *man's* world. Can you understand how I feel?"

The secretary shrugged. "It's a free country, sir. You're entitled to your own opinion . . . ."

"Of course I am," Stanley said. "We're all entitled to our own opinions. I'm glad to see you're on board, Miss Jones!"

The secretary glanced at her watch and smiled weakly. "Is that all you needed me for, Mr. Whitehead?"

"Yes, that's all. You may go to lunch now."

When Miss Jones had left, Stanley, his ordeal over and his mission apparently accomplished, plopped back down into his swivel chair and let out a sigh of relief.

That afternoon, as he went about his Senior Partnerly duties, Stanley felt a sense of peace and serenity he hadn't experienced for some time. Maybe, he thought—just maybe—the genteel atmosphere in which he had practiced law for so many years was about to make a comeback. Things that had been turned inside out would be turned outside in, and things turned upside down turned right side up.

Unfortunately, Stanley's euphoria was short-lived. Strolling through the parking garage on his way out, he noticed his new Mercedes listing to the side like a ship in distress taking on water. Approaching the vehicle with

76

trepidation, he discovered, to his chagrin, the left front tire spread over the concrete floor like a giant turd.

"Damnation!" he muttered to himself, clicking his remote key and popping open the trunk.

A half hour later, he could be seen sitting cross-legged on the garage floor, his face and hands covered with grease, wearing the expression of a little boy who has broken his favorite Christmas toy. Beside him lay the spare tire, a lug wrench, a disassembled jack and a copy of his owner's manual, open to the first page:

> Note: In this manual, every effort has been made to use gender neutral language. Where clarity requires, however, the masculine pronoun has been used. The reader should note that it refers to persons of either gender.

"Have a flat, Mr. Whitehead?" The Senior Partner looked up to see the concerned face of Doris Jones staring at him from beneath a checkered shawl.

"Oh, Miss Jones," he said breathlessly, his cheeks displaying a reddish tinge. "Yes, someone seems to have let the air out of my tire. It looks like it was punctured by a knife or some other sharp implement . . . ."

The secretary clucked her tongue disapprovingly. "My goodness, who would ever do such a thing?"

Grunting, Stanley lifted his aging frame from the concrete and dusted himself off. "Perhaps some juvenile hooligan. Or maybe even an unhappy staffer. Anyway, I haven't changed a tire in—I don't know how long—and, well, I'm not very handy at things like this. I wonder if I could trouble you to go back to the office and call Triple-A . . . ?"

Miss Jones pursed her lips. "Triple-A, sir? Oh, that will take much too long. Here, let me help you."

With that, the secretary removed her overcoat, jacket and shawl, rolled up her sleeves, crouched down and began assembling the jack.

"Oh, Miss Jones," Stanley pleaded, "don't trouble yourself. That's really not a job for a gentle lady like yourself."

While Stanley hovered over her like an anxious father-to-be in a hospital delivery room, and a crowd of curious onlookers gathered and gawked, she proceeded to hoist the car on the jack, remove the flat and mount the spare with the efficiency of a pit-crew mechanic in a 500–mile race.

The secretary continued on as if her boss had said nothing of consequence. While Stanley hovered over her like an anxious father-to-be in a hospital delivery room, and a crowd of curious onlookers gathered and gawked, she proceeded to hoist the car on the jack, remove the flat and mount the spare with the efficiency of a pit crew mechanic in a 500-mile race. She completed the task to the mild applause of the assembled spectators.

"All done," she chirped pleasantly as she slammed the door of the trunk shut. "Have a nice evening, sir."

Stanley was speechless. "Uh . . . er . . . uh . . . thank you, Miss Jones," he finally sputtered.

"My pleasure, Mr. Whitehead," she replied, donning her jacket. "It's all in a day's work."

Stanley finally gathered himself sufficiently to ask a question. "Tell me, Miss Jones, where did you learn to change a tire like that?"

The secretary laughed softly. "Why, from my mother, sir. She taught me all about cars, as well as how to fix a leaky faucet, how to assemble a new appliance, how to make repairs around the house—things like that. She believed that the world was in such disarray that a woman had to do everything herself just to make sure it was done right. 'Doris,' she would say, 'you have to learn to take care of yourself.'"

Stanley scratched his head. "Prudent counsel, I suppose, but perhaps a bit overstated. Why did she believe so strongly in female self-reliance?"

Miss Jones smiled coyly. "Because, sir—as you yourself have said many times—it's a man's world."

GARBAGE IN, GARBAGE OUT

"Planning, Miss Jones–planning is everything," observed a beaming Stanley Whitehead as he inspected the meticulously-labeled cardboard boxes stacked neatly outside his corner office. "It's something we lawyers are trained to do. And we're particularly good at it–don't you agree?"

"Yes, of course, Mr. Whitehead, whatever you say," the slim, silver-haired secretary replied as she got up from her desk, slung her handbag over her shoulder and prepared to leave for the three-day weekend.

"Indeed," the portly Senior Partner continued, tugging at his suspenders and rocking back and forth on his heels like a proud father boasting of a newborn baby, "greater planning has gone into this move than into a manned space shot. And my idea of moving over the Labor Day weekend is the key: everything shipped, delivered and unpacked before we open for business on Tuesday–a full six days ahead of schedule! An absolutely flawless scheme–don't you concur?"

"Well, Mr. Whitehead," Miss Jones said, her eyebrows arched, "you know what they say–'the best laid plans . . . .' I'm sure something will go awry. It always does."

"Nonsense! Don't be so negative, Miss Jones. I've arranged this move right down to the last legal pad. River City Transport has been instructed to take everything but the trash. In fact, I've approached this with the same skill and care that I use when counseling a client on the law. Nothing could possibly go wrong!"

The secretary shrugged. "All I can say, Mr. Whitehead, is don't forget that old saying about a lawyer representing himself having a fool for a client!"

Stanley dismissed the secretary's barb with an indifferent wave of the hand. In fact, so confident was he that things would proceed according to plan that he put the move out of his mind and took his wife, Katherine, to the shore for the long weekend.

When he arrived on Tuesday morning, Stanley conducted an inspection tour of the new offices. He was delighted at what he saw. It was as if the firm had been lifted up, carried across town and set down again, undisturbed, like a child's dollhouse moved from one room to another. Everything was exactly where it was supposed to be, from the imposing portrait of his late father on the lobby wall to the potted plants on the windowsills.

"Miss Jones, take a memo—To All":

"I wish to thank everyone for their patience and cooperation. As expected, our move went without a hitch, thanks in no small measure to the careful planning and 'hands-on' management for which our firm is noted. Everything required for the practice of law by Whitehead & Williams—'River City's Wall Street Law Firm'—is now in place."

After the secretary had finished typing the memo, Stanley scanned it quickly, then instructed her to send it out by e-mail. He crumpled up the draft and casually tossed it over his shoulder in the direction of the wastebasket. It landed on the plushly-carpeted floor.

"Miss Jones," he barked over the intercom, "where is my wastebasket? It's disappeared."

"Funny thing, Mr. Whitehead," she replied, "I don't seem to have a wastebasket either."

A hurried check of nearby offices soon revealed that the problem was universal. It seemed that everything had survived the move but the trash receptacles.

"Johnson, where the devil are our wastebaskets and garbage cans?" Stanley bellowed at the Manager of River City Transport over the phone.

"They're right where you wanted them, Mr. Whitehead," came the reply. "Back in your old offices. You told us to move everything but the trash . . . ."

There was a prolonged pause as the Senior Partner groped for the right words. "You moron," he finally sputtered, "I didn't mean the trash receptacles should be left behind–just their contents!"

"No problem, Mr. Whitehead. I'll send a crew over to pick them up. You should have them by, say, the end of the day tomorrow."

"Tomorrow? But we need them today!"

"No can do, Mr. W. You see, since you had us working on Labor Day, I had to give the boys the day off. Union rules, you know."

Stanley called Miss Jones into his office and explained the situation.

"But there's no need to panic," he said with a stiff smile. "It's nothing that can't be handled with a little creativity–the kind we lawyers apply when something unexpected comes up. First, we'll send out an e-mail informing the staff that, until further notice, empty shipping cartons should be used for trash . . . ."

"But, Mr. Whitehead," the secretary interrupted, "there aren't any empty shipping cartons. Don't you remember? You told the movers you wanted everything done by this morning–that you didn't want to see a single box or crate when you arrived. Apparently, they complied with your wishes."

The Senior Partner's smile dissolved into the anxious look of a jittery patient just informed that dentist will see him now. "But what are we going to do? A law office can't function without wastebaskets and garbage cans! You might as well take away our law licenses!"

"I've got an idea," she said, snapping her fingers and smiling brightly. "We'll just build our own garbage dump."

By noon, the resourceful secretary had converted the conference room next to her boss's office into a temporary waste disposal site, complete with trash bags, twist ties and a shredding machine. Throughout the day, as Stanley brooded behind closed doors, a seemingly endless parade of lawyers, secretaries, file clerks and messengers streamed past, loaded down with law office refuse–from drafts and extra copies of letters, memos, contracts and complaints to old newspapers and magazines and unwanted pencils, pens, paperclips and Post-It Notes. At two o'clock, the cafeteria staff arrived with the remnants of that day's lunch. By five-thirty, the conference room was filled to capacity with bulging, multicolored plastic bags.

"Just look at that, Miss Jones," Stanley moaned. "It's like a scene out of a horror movie–'The Invasion of the Giant Blobs'! If I didn't know better, I'd say this firm was in the business of churning out garbage. Thank God the cleaning crew will excise this eyesore tonight."

But the next morning the pile of trash bags remained. A call to the Building Superintendent (who had just returned from an extended Labor Day weekend) revealed the source of the problem.

"I didn't know you folks were in there," he explained. "I thought you weren't moving until this weekend. Anyway,

84

I need to hire two new people to handle your offices. I'll have them by, say, tomorrow night."

When Miss Jones entered her boss's office, he was sitting at his desk, grim-faced. "Miss Jones," he said, thoughtfully tapping a pencil against his forehead, "along with the necessity for careful planning and creativity, I've learned during my long career that patience is required for the successful practice of law–like when we have to endure protracted negotiations over a big contract or wait for a judge to issue an important ruling. We'll just have to tough this one out. You may now open the conference room on the other side of my office as an additional waste disposal site."

By late Thursday, mountains of garbage surrounded the Senior Partner. Trash bags oozed out into the hallway like congealing blood from an open wound. In spite of heavy doses of air freshener and scented insect repellent (required to ward off an incipient infestation of roaches), the unmistakable fragrance of rotting food filled the air, converting Stanley's corner of the new office into a toxic no-man's land.

"Miss Jones, in addition to planning, creativity and patience," the Senior Partner sighed as he packed up his briefcase and prepared to depart for the day, "I've learned that a lawyer sometimes has to accept temporary setbacks–like when we lose at a trial but win on appeal. And, as difficult as it is, I do so in this case. But at least this trash will be out of here by tomorrow and things will be back to normal."

It was therefore with trepidation that the secretary explained the situation the next morning to her near-catatonic boss.

"Recycling, Mr. Whitehead. According to the Building Manager, our lease requires us to separate paper, bottles and cans from all our other trash. He told me that you agreed to this in exchange for a reduction in the maintenance charge. Anyway, that's why the cleaning crew refused to take the garbage out last night."

The Senior Partner groaned, emitting the forlorn sound of a deflating balloon.

Despite mutterings of "is this why I went to law school?", the trio of strapping young men succeeded in clearing the office of all waste by noon. "The firm won't forget this come bonus time," Stanley assured them as the disheveled and disgruntled associates trudged away with the last of the trash bags in tow.

"But don't worry, I've already asked River City Hauling to bring over a dumpster right away. And I've also asked our three most junior lawyers to come up immediately. I told them you had an assignment for them."

Despite mutterings of "is this why I went to law school?", the trio of strapping young men succeeded in clearing the office of all waste by noon. "The firm won't forget this come bonus time," Stanley assured them as the disheveled and disgruntled associates trudged away with the last of the trash bags in tow.

"Well, Miss Jones, I'm leaving for the day," Stanley announced, closing the conference room doors to prevent the further escape of the lingering stench. "It's been a trying week. But, in the practice of law, I guess you live and learn. Don't you agree?"

"I do, Mr. Whitehead. And it's interesting how you're able to apply what you've learned as a lawyer to everyday problems. But I think you've overlooked something."

Stanley gazed quizzically at the secretary. "I have? What?"

"Well, with recycling, we'll need three times as many wastebaskets and trash cans as we have now."

The Senior Partner's face turned ashen. "Oh, God, no," he moaned, staggering backward. "I didn't think of that."

The secretary grabbed her boss by the arm to steady him.

"Don't worry, Mr. Whitehead," she said, "I've taken care of it. River City Office Supplies promises to have everything we need over here by early this afternoon, and I've already sent an e-mail around instructing everyone about the new waste disposal system. Now just go home and enjoy your weekend. You deserve it."

Stanley sighed the sigh of a condemned man just handed a reprieve. "Miss Jones, I don't know what I'd do without you."

"Why, thank you so much. But, of course, I do have one advantage over you, sir."

"Really? What's that, Miss Jones?"

The secretary smiled. "I wasn't trained as a lawyer!"

INTERVENTION

Doris Jones, her silver hair streaming down her shoulders, her steel-rimmed spectacles perched atop her head, marched into Stanley Whitehead's corner office, shut the door behind her and strode up to his enormous mahogany desk. Arms folded, she glared at her boss like an angry client kept waiting in the lobby.

"*Mister Whitehead*," she huffed, tapping her foot on the carpeting, "when are you going to do something about Jonathan Hayes? You promised you would."

Looking up from the memo he was reading, Stanley gazed at the secretary, completely baffled. "Miss Jones, what are you talking about?"

The secretary shook her head in dismay. "Don't you remember our conversation, sir — the one we had almost a month ago?"

Stanley furrowed his brow pensively. The answer finally dawned on him.

"Ah . . . yes . . . Mr. Hayes," he said, fidgeting with his mustache and clearing his throat. "I've been meaning to have a chat with him, but, what with one thing and another . . . . And, you know how it is when you get busy. The Senior Partner's work is never done!"

Stanley's evasive answer didn't satisfy the persistent secretary. "Mr. Whitehead, Denise O'Connor and I just rode up with the man on the elevator. By the time we arrived on our floor, we felt as if we'd spent the afternoon in Kelly's Bar and Grill. See, you can smell it on me!" she added, offering up the sleeve of her white cotton blouse for Stanley's olfactory inspection.

The Senior Partner summarily brushed her arm away. "I suppose, Miss Jones, that, by 'it,' you mean some form of alcoholic beverage. You think Mr. Hayes may have had one too many at lunch . . . ?"

"One too many? Try four or five."

Stanley rose to his feet and began pacing back and forth, his hands clasped behind his back, like a law professor about to explain some esoteric legal principle to the class. "Now, now, I'm sure you're exaggerating. After all, many lawyers need a bracer during the day. Our practice can be stressful . . . ."

"But that isn't what we're talking about here. Just yesterday, I saw Mr. Hayes coming out of the men's room at eleven o'clock in the morning with a pint bottle sticking out of his jacket pocket. And it wasn't Listerine!"

"I won't dispute what you saw," Stanley reluctantly conceded. "But he may be having problems at home, or with his health. Plus, as far as I can tell, he isn't hurting anyone . . . ."

Miss Jones looked up toward the ceiling as if seeking divine guidance. "Mr. Whitehead, the man has a disease! He needs help. It's time you stopped making excuses for him and did something about it—like organize an intervention."

A puzzled expression crossed Stanley's face. "A what?"

"An intervention. That's where friends, family and co-workers get together, under the guidance of a professional counselor, and confront an alcoholic about his drinking and the effect it's having on those around him. They're often held in the workplace . . . ."

Stanley signaled "Time Out." "Just hold on, Miss Jones. You're not the Senior Partner around here. I am. And this is my call. Now, before you go organizing one of these so-called 'interventions,' I think I should have a talk, mano a mano, with Jonathan."

The secretary sighed. "He needs more than just a talking to from the boss. Besides, you're not really qualified . . . ."

"Nonsense!" Stanley insisted. "As his superior and a fellow lawyer, I'm just the person who can set him straight. I'll speak to him at the earliest opportunity — I promise."

~ ~

Unfortunately, Stanley's earliest opportunity did not materialize until a reception held two weeks later to celebrate the opening of the firm's new offices.

At first, the carefully-orchestrated event, held in the ornately appointed library, went according to plan. With over two hundred guests present, the firm put on a show worthy of a Hollywood premiere, the dedication of a new dam or the launching of a battleship. Even Jack Lewis, the Chairman of arch-rivals, Lewis & Lamb, was impressed by the show ("Really puttin' on the Ritz, eh, Stanley?" he needled the Senior Partner. "What did you do — dip into your client trust funds?") Things were going so well, in fact, that Stanley completely forgot about the unfortunate incident of the wastebaskets and garbage cans that had marred the firm's move to its new quarters.

Then, Jonathan Hayes burst upon the scene like a deadbeat relative at a family reunion.

As the Senior Partner watched in horror, his boyish-looking partner suddenly took upon himself the role of unofficial master of ceremonies. Wide-eyed and bubbly, a wine glass in one hand and a bottle of White Zinfandel in the other, Hayes hoisted himself onto a conference table before the collection of blue-chip guests, called for order and then, with a stupid grin upon his face, launched into a fifteen-minute comedy monologue, consisting mainly of old lawyer jokes, awkward double-entendres and inadvertent belches.

Staggering from one end of the table to the other, listing dangerously from side to side like a freighter in distress,

Wide-eyed and bubbly, a wine glass in one hand and a bottle of White Zinfandel in the other, Hayes hoisted himself onto a conference table before the collection of blue-chip guests, called for order and then, with a stupid grin upon his face, launched into a fifteen-minute comedy monologue, consisting mainly of old lawyer jokes, awkward double-entendres and inadvertent belches.

Hayes demonstrated himself to be a stand-up comic of modest talent, if not a lawyer of particularly good taste and judgment. He climbed down from his perch only when it became evident that he was losing his audience.

"*Now* will you speak to him?" Doris Jones chided Stanley as the unsteady partner took his final bow.

The next morning, a bleary-eyed Jonathan Hayes, dressed in the same crumpled brown suit he'd worn the night before, his blond hair in disarray, sat passively in Stanley's office, a hang-dog expression on his unshaven face.

"Well, Jonathan, what do you have to say for yourself?" Stanley asked his partner.

"I'm sorry, Stanley," the downtrodden lawyer replied. "Last night's performance was clearly out of line. I don't know what comes over me sometimes. It's scary!"

"It certainly was that!"

Stanley didn't know quite what to say next. He decided to take a "soft sell" approach to his wayward colleague.

"Well, I suppose it can happen to the best of us," he said, cracking a stiff smile. "Why, I remember back in my days at Phi Delta Gamma, I could act pretty silly at a Friday night beer blast . . . ."

"That wasn't a fraternity party, Stanley," Hayes interrupted, almost as if he were challenging the senior lawyer's judgment. "I wasn't being hazed."

"And, for a while there," Stanley went on, dismissing the remark with a hollow laugh, "you did have your audience in stitches."

The young partner, startled by this comment, stirred uncomfortably in his chair. "But were they laughing with me or at me, Stanley? You know, I've always told myself that I don't have a problem—that I can control my drinking, quit any time I want to. But now, I'm not sure. Maybe I'm an . . . an . . . alcoholic."

Stanley winced, as if Hayes had just uttered some crude profanity. "Don't talk that way," he said. "After all, you're a successful attorney, you haven't lost your family and friends, and you're not wallowing around in the gutter like a common derelict. And," he added, not quite knowing why, "nobody's asking you to quit—just to ease up for a bit—exercise some restraint. Now will you promise me that—as a friend?"

Hayes seemed puzzled. "Uh...er...I appreciate the vote of confidence, Stanley. I'll cut down. You can trust me. I promise!"

When Hayes had left, Miss Jones stuck her head into Stanley's office. "Well, how did it go, sir?"

Feeling stalked by the secretary, the Senior Partner looked up and smiled innocently. "Just fine, Miss Jones. Everything's been taken care of. You won't have to worry about Mr. Hayes anymore."

Turning to the morning mail, Stanley thought he saw, out of the corner of his eye, a troubled expression on the secretary's face.

For awhile, Stanley's appeal to moderation seemed to work. From the reports he received from others in the office, no longer could the young partner be found seated at the Oyster Bar in the River City Club, sipping gin-and-tonics at noon, or on a stool at the Ritz Bar, sampling fine wine after work. At Firm functions, he'd taken to imbibing Perrier rather than Port.

"You see, Miss Jones," Stanley remarked one day as the two passed through the line in the cafeteria, "there's Jonathan Hayes with a glass of orange juice on his tray. Our little talk seems to have done some good. Lawyers are always willing to listen to reason."

The secretary pursed her lips. "You may be right, sir, but
. . . ."

"No 'buts,' Miss Jones," Stanley grunted, doing his best
imitation of a no-nonsense boss.

The following afternoon, however, the secretary crept
into Stanley's office to deliver a dose of bad news.

"Mr. Whitehead, do you have a moment?"

"Yes, of course."

The secretary slowly seated herself, her eyes downcast.
"I'm not sure how to tell you this. But I just took a call for
you from Judge Brown's clerk. He told me that . . . that Mr.
Hayes is in jail."

Stanley dropped his pencil onto the floor. "In jail? Is this
some sort of joke?"

The secretary shook her head. "Apparently, the Judge
had him taken into custody when he . . . he made an
obscene gesture in chambers after losing a motion. He was
cited for contempt and taken to the City Lock-Up
to . . . uh . . . to dry out."

Later that afternoon, Stanley was admitted to the drunk
tank at the City Jail to retrieve his junior partner from
custody. Seated on a wooden bench behind iron bars,
thrown in among a horde of sullen and hostile-looking
men, a bewildered Jonathan Hayes stared blankly into
space, looking as if he'd lost his best friend.

"Jonathan, how could you do something like this?"
Stanley demanded of the lawyer as the two sat in the
interview room following Hayes release into the Senior
Partner's custody. "You promised you were going to
control your drinking!"

The young man put his head in his hands and wearily
rubbed his eyes. "I know. And, for a while, I kept my
promise. In fact, I went a whole month limiting myself to

three drinks a day. Then, because I'd done so well, I thought a little celebration might be in order, so this afternoon, after lunch . . . ."

The chastened lawyer paused and sighed. "Oh, what's the use? I'm a drunk, pure and simple. I ought to check myself into rehab. It would be best for everyone."

Stanley glanced anxiously around the room, as if the two were under surveillance. Satisfied that they were not, he put his arm around Hayes's shoulders and laid down the party line.

"Jonathan, old friend," he cajoled, "what on earth are you talking about? You don't need rehab. You need self-control. Besides, what if word got out that one of our partners was an alcoholic? Lawyers can't have drinking problems; we can't have drunks at Whitehead & Williams. I'd rather see you blotto in the office than sober in detox. Trust me!"

Stanley paused. "But you will have to go on the wagon," he added as a clarifying afterthought. "At least for the indefinite future."

Hayes gazed up like a child told that he won't receive a spanking after all. "Thank you, Stanley," he said, wiping his now-parched lips with the back of his hand. "You're a good man. This time I won't let you down. I swear."

Judge Brown—an old friend and golfing buddy of Stanley's—agreed to expunge the inebriated attorney's infraction from the record on condition that the Senior Partner guarantee to keep him out of trouble. Later, when several lawyers asked about a rumor they'd heard of the incident, Stanley, adhering as always to the strict truth, replied that he had no idea how rumors of that nature got started.

"I think we've dodged a bullet, Miss Jones," Stanley confided to the secretary after two weeks had passed without inquiry from the state bar authorities, the news media or other law firms.

"You may have dodged a bullet, sir, but are you sure you don't have a loose cannon on deck?"

This was the secretary's last thought on the subject until the afternoon of the accident.

According to the police report, Jonathan Hayes didn't explain the collision in the parking garage like other drunk drivers. He didn't say that the accident wasn't his fault; he didn't maintain that the brand new Mercedes he'd struck was improperly parked, or that his brakes had failed, or that a broken overhead light had obscured his vision; and he didn't claim that his speedometer was stuck at forty-two miles an hour in a five-mile-an-hour zone because of the impact of the collision. He simply told the cops he was drunk.

"My car!" Stanley moaned to Doris Jones, kicking aside a detached rear fender as the injured perpetrator was sped away in an ambulance. "Why did he have to trash my car?"

"Don't take it personally, sir," the secretary replied, patting her boss on the arm like a kindly aunt. "You just have to realize that Mr. Hayes is not in control of his drinking. He needs the help of others."

Stanley shook his head, half in disgust, half in resignation. "I don't know what he needs, but I suppose we have to do something. Why don't you call Doctor Andreas and have him contact me after I get back from Chicago. Maybe we can come up with an idea — like one of those interventions you spoke to me about."

The secretary smiled weakly. "I'll see what I can do, sir."

~ ~

Three days later, after returning from Chicago, Stanley sat in his office with Doris Jones, grumbling about the havoc that Jonathan Hayes was wreaking on his life.

"I've been thinking about how I'm going to approach Jonathan," the Senior Partner said. "Sort of a combination of the carrot and the stick—good cop, bad cop—tough love and all that. What do you think, Miss Jones?"

The secretary coughed daintily, then repositioned herself on her chair. "Well, Mr. Whitehead," she said, screwing her face into a smile, "you really don't have to worry about what you're going to say."

Stanley started. "What? Why not? I thought you said we should hold an intervention. We probably should arrange one as soon as possible. Perhaps sometime . . . er . . . next week. And certainly my thoughts will be vital if we're to keep Jonathan away from the bottle. I should at least be telling him that he's lucky I'm giving him another chance."

Miss Jones scratched her head. "Well, Mr. Whitehead, the truth is we've already had the intervention—yesterday, at the hospital, with Mrs. Hayes, their children and many friends and colleagues there. The doctors felt that we ought to speak with him right away, before he was discharged. It was strange, though. He didn't resist, like most alcoholics do. He agreed to go into rehab without a fuss—as if he'd known all along that he was an alcoholic, and was just waiting for someone to confirm it."

Stanley felt an uncomfortable burning sensation in the pit of his stomach. "Well, I didn't authorize any intervention," he said, a tad defensively. "And I certainly didn't approve of holding one without my participation. Why didn't the doctors wait until I got back?"

"Actually, Mr. Whitehead, they said that it really wasn't necessary that you participate."

Stanley scowled. "And why was that, Miss Jones?"

"They said you'd intervened enough already," the secretary replied.

Stanley suddenly felt like a kid told that he hasn't made the little league team. "Oh," he muttered.

"Anyway, Mr. Hayes agreed that I should serve as his liaison with the lawyers here at the firm, including you. I think he's going to be alright."

Stanley nodded in agreement. "Well, I suppose the doctors know best, and that we'll have to let the chips fall where they may. But you will keep me informed concerning Jonathan's progress, won't you, Miss Jones?"

The secretary, a look of surprise on her face, smiled slyly. "Of course I will, Mr. Whitehead. I'll keep you fully informed. You can trust me. I promise!"

THE BOSS

"Thank you so much, Mr. Whitehead," warbled Doris Jones, as she squeezed herself behind the postage stamp-size table. "You're a most thoughtful boss."

"Think nothing of it, Miss Jones," the Senior Partner replied. "I simply wanted to recognize your years of dedicated service to the firm. Besides, it's National Secretary's Day."

"And to think," she continued, ducking to avoid a tray full of dirty dishes wielded by a passing busboy, "that you arranged everything yourself — the flowers, the nice card and, most of all, this wonderful lunch."

Stanley cleared his throat. "I apologize about the flowers. I didn't know you were allergic . . . .

"Oh, that's alright, sir. You couldn't possibly have known: after all, in twenty years, you've never once bought me flow . . . . I mean, it's the thought that counts."

Just then, a blue-coated waiter, precariously balancing plate loads of mixed green salad on his arm, shot out the kitchen door like a panic-stricken fire victim fleeing a burning building. Failing to see Stanley's outstretched leg, he went flying forward, falling flat on his face.

Heads turned, and a collective gasp arose from nearby tables.

"Terribly sorry," Stanley said nonchalantly as the waiter picked himself up off the floor.

"Are you alright, Michael?" asked the Maitre D', rushing to the assistance of the fallen server.

"It's nothing," the waiter replied, as he wiped gobs of French dressing off his trousers with a napkin and cast a hostile glance at Stanley.

Just then, a blue-coated waiter, precariously balancing plate loads of mixed green salad on his arm, shot out the kitchen door like a panic-stricken fire victim fleeing a burning building. Failing to see Stanley's outstretched leg, he went flying forward, falling flat on his face.

"My fault, Maurice," confessed the lawyer. "Of course," he added defensively, "it was an accident waiting to happen. It would never have occurred had you seated us somewhere other than by the kitchen door."

"My apologies, sir," said the Maitre D' with a waxen smile. "But you didn't make your reservation until after eleven, when all the other tables had been taken. Usually, your secretary — a Miss Jones, I believe her name is — calls promptly at nine to arrange for a table. She's very efficient, you know."

A sheepish grin crossed Stanley's face. "How rude of me. Maurice, let me introduce Miss Jones."

The Maitre D's eyes lit up as he gazed at the silver-haired secretary. "You are Miss Jones — *the* Miss Jones?" he asked, as if suddenly finding himself in the presence of a legendary star of stage and screen. "It is indeed an honor to meet you." He bowed awkwardly, seizing her hand and planting a kiss on it.

The secretary blushed. "Maurice, you're too kind."

"Oh, had I only known you would be gracing us with your presence . . . ." He straightened his jacket, raised his hand in the air and snapped his fingers.

"Alice," he commanded a young woman standing guard at the entrance, " — a more suitable table for Mr. Whitehead and his guest!"

Within a minute, the attorney and his secretary were comfortably ensconced in a dimly-lit corner booth.

"Seems you wield a good deal of influence around here, Miss Jones," Stanley said as they scanned their menus. "You get the best table in the house. I get the equivalent of a bench at Grand Central!"

"Oh, don't be silly, sir. It's my job to take care of the details — like making restaurant reservations, ordering cabs, booking hotel rooms — so you can focus on what you do best — practicing law."

Stanley was mollified until the main course arrived.

"I specifically told them not to put Hollandaise sauce on the broccoli!" he grumbled after the waiter had left.

"Dr. Andreas would shoot me if he caught me shoveling all that fat and cholesterol down my gullet."

The secretary, finishing a delicate chew of a small carrot, signaled the Maitre D'. The harried host ran over to the table, a concerned expression on his face. "Yes, Miss Jones?"

"Maurice," she said sternly, "your chef is trying to poison Mr. Whitehead. He explicitly said *'no Hollandaise sauce!'*"

The Maitre D's face turned bright red. "Again, I'm terribly sorry. I'll take care of it right away."

Later, Miss Jones similarly rescued Stanley when he was served cherry cobbler rather than the bowl of cherries he'd ordered, and when the waiter poured regular coffee into the cup from which he'd expected to imbibe decaf.

By the time the check arrived, Stanley was more than ready to return to the office.

"Well, at least the bill is reasonable," he said, extracting a credit card from his wallet and tossing it onto the tray.

Miss Jones clucked her tongue disapprovingly. "Sir, the restaurant has stopped accepting American Express. They called me about it last week."

A sorrowful look crossed the Senior Partner's face, like that of a small boy who's been told that the ice cream man has run out of his favorite flavor. "They don't take American Express?" he whined. "Why didn't you tell me? You know it's the only card I carry with me. And I didn't bring any cash . . . ."

The secretary smiled. "I sent you an e-mail about it, sir. But don't fret. I'll see what I can do."

With that, she rose from the table and approached the Maitre D'. Stanley, his mouth dry, watched as the two whispered to each other—like crafty and cunning conspirators—periodically glancing and pointing in his direction.

"No problem, sir," she chirped pleasantly when she returned. "Maurice will accept your check."

"Why shouldn't he take my check," Stanley thundered. "I have lunch here all the time!"

"Calm down, Mr. Whitehead," the secretary cautioned. "You don't want to have a stroke. And, oh, please make the check out to me; I'll endorse it over to the restaurant. Seems they want me on the hook for it."

Later, as Stanley opened the front door for the secretary, the two were greeted by a flash of lightening, followed by a burst of thunder. "Funny," Stanley remarked, turning up his collar, "I don't remember the weatherman saying anything about rain."

Driving back to the office, Stanley—his suit soaking wet—contemplated his complete humiliation. "If the valet hadn't parked the car three blocks away, we could have avoided that little downpour."

"Mea culpa," the secretary said. "When I make the reservations, I always call ahead to make sure they reserve a parking space for you nearby. But it was fortunate that the attendant had an umbrella. Too bad we both couldn't fit under it."

Stanley smiled weakly. "I've learned my lesson, Miss Jones. I ought to leave everything up to you. You surely know how to get things done. I owe you!"

The secretary laughed. "Well, thank you, sir. I just try to do my job. But, now that you mention it, there was something Maurice mentioned to me . . . ."

Back in the office, Miss Jones placed a call to the Maitre D'.

"Thanks for everything, Maury," she said. "This should help come bonus time. At least now he appreciates everything I do for him."

"Think nothing of it, Dory."

"Perhaps the thunderstorm was a bit much . . . ."

"Well, I can't take credit for the weather. But, tell me, is your firm going to represent my brother's new Internet business?"

"He agreed as soon as we got back. 'You're the boss,' he says. Oh, I hate to take advantage of the poor man. He's a bit pompous, but well-meaning . . . and so gullible!"

The Maitre D' suddenly turned serious. "Don't waste your sympathies on that guy, Dory. We peons have to stick together. It's the only way things ever get done."

There was a pause. "Yes . . . I suppose you're right," she replied with a muted sigh.

THE SYSTEM

Stanley Whitehead had run out of excuses. Despite his high-level connections on the Bench and at the Bar, he could no longer avoid his civic duty. This time around, the system had spurned his pleas of hardship and indispensability as so much hokum. Like a convicted felon who'd exhausted his appeals, he had to do his time.

"Oh, Stanley, calm down and eat your bran flakes," his wife, Katherine, chided that Monday morning as he paced nervously back and forth in the kitchen, preparing to go down to the courthouse for his day of reckoning. "You know as well as I do that lawyers never get picked for juries. The attorneys are too worried that you'll second-guess them — or, worse, second-guess the judge. They'll never permit you to serve on a panel."

Stanley glared at his wife. "But that's the problem," he said. "What you're saying is that I'm about to waste two weeks of my life sitting on my keister at that decrepit courthouse, doing nothing of any use to anyone. And I'm supposed to play golf with Hi Brown Friday in the Children's Aid Society Tournament."

"I thought Judge Brown was out of the country?"

"He is. But he gets back Wednesday night. Unfortunately, he's unreachable until then. And, by that time, it may be too late!"

Katherine shook her head, then brushed a speck of dandruff off Stanley's shoulder and straightened his tie, like a mother fussing over a son departing for the junior prom. "Well, I wouldn't worry about it. They'll probably get so sick and tired of your grumbling that they'll toss you out of the courthouse by the end of the day. I know I would!"

"I should be so lucky," Stanley grunted, grabbing his briefcase and heading toward the door, his bran flakes untouched.

~ ~

"Listen up people," barked the jury supervisor, a burly, bull-necked gentleman with an unpleasant demeanor and the raspy voice of a frustrated drill sergeant. "I'm only going to say this once. If you think you don't belong here—if you think you should be excused—go down to Room 506 and tell your story to them. Do *not* bother me with it."

Sitting with a horde of other prospective jurors in the musty jury assembly room, wearing a clip-on badge identifying him only as Juror 2281, Stanley turned to an elderly man seated next to him who was, at that moment, occupied examining the dirt under his fingernails. "I really ought to be excused," he said. "I'm an attorney, you know, and attorneys are never selected for juries. This is a complete waste of time!"

The man shrugged and muttered something in Spanish. Stanley nodded and thanked him in his native tongue.

Stanley spent the balance of the morning slumped in an uncomfortable green vinyl chair undergoing "jury orientation" (a euphemism, he thought, for brainwashing). Decked out in his best three-piece suit and wing-tipped shoes, he stood out from his fellow jurors—most of whom had arrived clad in comfortable slacks or shorts, tee-shirts and sneakers or sandals—like a distant relative at an extended family reunion. His bulky briefcase, stuffed with work from the office, clashed with the paperback books, tabloid newspapers, fan magazines, CD players and portable radios brought by others. I don't belong here, he thought to himself.

That afternoon, following a solitary lunch of dry roast beef, cold mashed potatoes and watery coffee in the courthouse's dingy basement cafeteria, Stanley tried to occupy himself with legal busywork. Soon bored to distraction, he decided, out of morbid curiosity, to read the jury service pamphlet handed out during orientation.

With its "Dick and Jane" explanation of the judicial system (complete with full-color illustrations of smiling judges, animated attorneys and diligent jurors), it was somewhat less inspiring than the Declaration of Independence or the Gettysburg Address. Nevertheless, as Stanley read on, he found himself warming to its message of civic duty. In spite of the hardships he was suffering, the words gave him a new perspective on things.

These simple words caused Stanley to pause and reflect.

> Jury service is both a sacred privilege and a solemn duty [the pamphlet said], and, when performed conscientiously, is a mark of good citizenship. As a juror, you play a key role in our democracy. Your service is greatly appreciated by the courts, our community and our entire society. The system could not function without you.

He thought back to his high school days, where, in Civics, he'd absorbed the sacred shibboleths of Good Citizenship (and, with a little editorial assistance from his father, won an Honorable Mention in a state-sponsored essay contest on the subject). Maybe jury service was worthwhile, he told himself. After all, his very presence at the courthouse was an act of civic responsibility, like voting and paying taxes. And why else had he become a lawyer, if not to serve the public? Besides, the legal system had been good to him, and it was high time to give something back. And, maybe—just maybe—he stood a chance of being selected for a jury panel. In fact, the possibility of serving on a jury, however remote, appealed to Stanley, whose deskbound career had always left him yearning for a taste of the courtroom action he'd seen on TV dramas and read about in legal thrillers.

Taking the pamphlet home in his briefcase that night, Stanley vowed to keep an open mind.

～ ～

The next morning, Stanley and some forty other prospective jurors were summoned to Department 125, Superior Court, for empanelment before Judge Lewis B. Stone.

Having forsaken his suit for casual slacks and a sports jacket, and his briefcase for a paperback novel, Stanley took his place on the hard wooden benches in the rear of the courtroom. When Judge Stone—a tall, distinguished-looking man with wavy white hair and piercing gray eyes—entered, and the Bailiff barked "All Rise," the Senior Partner snapped to attention like a green army recruit being mustered into service.

The case involved an attempted murder. "Those of you selected for the panel," the Judge explained as he surveyed the prospective jurors, "will be entrusted with the awesome task of deciding whether the defendant will be set free or sent to prison. Yet even those of you not selected will be contributing to the outcome of this case. Your presence here will ensure that justice is done."

Overnight, Stanley had decided he wanted to serve. When he'd told Katherine of his decision, she had reacted in her usual blunt fashion.

"I've been waiting for mid-life crisis to set in, Stanley, but this is a bit abrupt! Should I make an appointment with a therapist?"

Stanley squirmed as anxiously as a toddler in a barber's chair as the Judge questioned the other jurors. As he asked their names, residences, marital status, education, occupations and prior criminal records, Stanley mentally rehearsed his own answers to these questions. But, when called to the jury box, he was as tongue-tied as a drunk driver pulled over for speeding.

"My name is Stanley Whitehead, your Honor — that is, R. Stanley Whitehead, III. I live in River City . . . uh . . . River Grove . . . uh . . . with my wife and three children — well, actually, all of my children are grown and have moved away. Although my daughter, Melissa, works at my firm . . . . I'm a lawyer . . . that is, an attorney . . . ."

The youthful prosecuting attorney, who, up to that point, had been furiously taking notes, suddenly looked up, wide-eyed, from his legal pad, as if a fire alarm had gone off in the courtroom. The seedily-dressed defense lawyer, awakened from a momentary nap at the counsel table, whispered something to his client.

"I know who you are, Juror 2281," interrupted Judge Stone. "You're a most distinguished member of the local Bar. Welcome."

"Thank you, your Honor," Stanley replied, feeling relieved at this gesture of recognition.

"And we're honored to have you in court today. You know, we don't get many prominent lawyers in here — they usually manage to duck jury duty."

Stanley turned red as titters of nervous laughter filled the courtroom.

"Now, Juror 2281, for the record and the benefit of counsel, tell the Court what type of law you practice."

"Business law," Stanley announced proudly. "Corporations, securities, commercial contracts . . . ."

"A white shoe lawyer, eh?" the Judge parried with a smile. "A mouthpiece for the corporate fat cats and the Malefactors of Great Wealth."

Stanley nervously cleared his throat. "Some may say that," he said defensively. "But I prefer to think of myself as an advocate of the public interest."

His response was greeted by an eruption of derisive laughter, led by the prosecuting attorney and defense counsel. "Quiet!" shouted the Bailiff.

"Well, however you think of yourself, Juror 2281," the Judge went on, a friendly grin on his face, "you probably haven't had any exposure to ordinary criminal law since law school—except, of course, for what you've learned from the media, or read in popular novels—like the one you're holding in your hand. Is that correct?"

"That is correct, your Honor," Stanley said, awkwardly returning the paperback to his jacket pocket.

"And, if you are selected to serve, Juror 2281," continued the Judge, abruptly taking on a solemn tone, "will you decide this case fairly on the basis of the evidence presented and the law as I explain it to you—not as you think it is—or should be?"

"Yes, your Honor."

"I think I've got a shot at it," Stanley bubbled to Katherine, calling her on his cell phone during a recess. "I'm sure the Deputy State's Attorney wants me—he probably thinks my conservative background will favor the prosecution. But I think I've also convinced the defense attorney that I'm an independent-minded person who can give his client a fair shake."

112

"Whatever you say, darling," came the half-hearted reply. "But don't get your hopes up . . . ."

After the recess, peremptory challenges began. The prosecutor went first.

"Your Honor, the People request that the Court thank and excuse Juror 2281."

Stanley cringed, feeling as if he'd stumbled over a land mine.

"Juror 2281, you're excused. I direct you to return to the jury assembly room."

As Stanley shuffled out of the jury box, stepping on toes along the way, Judge Stone leaned over the bench and smiled. "And Juror 2281, the Court thanks you for your diligence and devotion—as well as for your sense of humor. I think I speak for the State's Attorney and defense counsel when I say that your willingness to serve has made us proud to be members of the Bar."

Stanley suddenly felt like a first-year law student discovering an "A+" at the top of an exam paper. Rejuvenated, he strode from the courtroom, his head held high.

Over the next twenty-four hours, Stanley was summoned in three other cases. One ended with a plea bargain. The other two followed the pattern of the first. When he identified himself as an attorney, heads bobbed at the counsel table and notations were made on legal pads. During peremptory challenges, the judge thanked and excused him.

By Wednesday afternoon, only two of the original jury pool remained—the elderly Spanish-speaking gentleman and the Senior Partner. Everyone else had been selected for a panel. But Stanley was undaunted, confident his time would come.

"Give it up, Stanley," Katherine said that evening as the two sat in their den watching "Twelve Angry Men" on home video. "Jury selection is like choosing partners at a grade school dance. If you're not popular, you're not picked. And lawyers are not popular. They're professional wallflowers. You can't buck the system, darling."

Before Stanley could respond, the phone rang. It was Hiram Brown.

"Stanley, I just got back from Nepal and, having conquered the Himalayas, I'm ready to kick some serious butt out at Riverdale! Are we still on for Friday?"

Stanley had completely forgotten about the Children's Aid Society Tournament. "I'm sorry, Hi, but I'm on jury duty — er, at least I'm waiting to be selected for a panel. I've got another week left to go. I can't shirk my responsibilities, you know."

"Baloney," the Judge barked. "Your responsibilities are to me, your golfing partner. I'll just have to spring you. I'll arrange it first thing tomorrow."

"But Hi . . . ." Judge Brown had already hung up.

When Stanley arrived at the courthouse the following morning, the supervisor reassigned him to a new jury pool. "It really doesn't matter," the lawyer said with a tinge of frustration, taking his seat and opening up his paperback. "I'll be gone by noon."

"We'll see about that," the supervisor replied, cackling almost demonically. "I'm sending you all down to City

Court for empanelment (or should I say, 'impalement') before Commissioner Schwartz!"

Before the Commissioner stretched a seemingly endless line of supplicants — each seeking an audience with the aged jurist — bumping and jostling one another like hassled travelers fighting at a ticket counter to get a seat on the last flight to Buffalo.

Within fifteen minutes, Stanley entered the dimly-lit, ground-floor hovel of Myron O. Schwartz, Commissioner of the City Court, known in local Bar circles as "Old Shoot from the Hip." As a judge of the "lower" courts, the octogenarian Commissioner handled everything from small claims and misdemeanors to domestic disputes and minor traffic violations. Surveying his crowded quarters, Stanley felt as if he'd mistakenly wandered into a busy airport terminal on Christmas Eve. Before the Commissioner stretched a seemingly endless line of supplicants — each seeking an audience with the aged jurist — bumping and jostling one another like hassled travelers fighting at a ticket counter to get a seat on the last flight to Buffalo.

"It's motions and pleas day," explained the Bailiff, as he led Stanley and the other prospective jurors to their seats through the tangle of lawyers, parties and witnesses. "I'm afraid you'll have to wait."

Stanley watched in amazement as the diminutive Commissioner dispatched the business of the court with the ruthless efficiency of a Star Chamber Deputy. "Motion denied," "Sixty days in the City Lock-Up," "Fifty dollars," "Case dismissed," "Time served and six months probation," "Continuance denied" and "Next case" seemed to be the limit of his vocabulary. Each utterance was followed by a firm rap of the gavel, accompanied by a forbidding scowl.

"Okay," the Commissioner thundered, as the last applicant withdrew from the bench. "Case 98-45342 — People versus Wyzanski."

In less than a minute, the Bailiff had escorted Stanley and eleven other prospective jurors into the jury box. A prosecution for petty theft, the defendant, a tiny, frail, elderly lady — a bewildered look on her care-worn face — stood accused of shoplifting two tubes of lipstick and a bottle of nail polish from a local K-Mart.

Commissioner Schwartz peppered the jurors with questions like a malfunctioning machine gun. When he got around to Stanley, he made all the standard inquiries — all, that is, except for his occupation — which he apparently overlooked in his haste.

116

During a brief recess, Stanley paced nervously outside the courtroom, watching the young City Attorney make a hurried call on a pay phone. He still had hope that he would be selected. After all, lawyers practicing in the bowels of the municipal court system probably wouldn't recognize him, and the Commissioner didn't seem to care who you were as long as you had a pulse. And, once he was selected, it would be too late for Hi Brown to spring him from service!

As he waited to be called back, Stanley tried to imagine what it would be like to serve on the jury — sitting in the jury box, listening to testimony, viewing exhibits, hearing motions and objections, being instructed on the law, retiring to deliberate, being selected as Foreman, sifting through the evidence, explaining the law to his fellow jurors, developing a consensus on guilt or innocence — and, finally, delivering the verdict on behalf of the jury.

"Mr. Foreman, has the jury reached a verdict?"

"We have, your Honor. 'We, the jurors in the above-entitled action, find the defendant . . . .'"

"Prospective jurors should return to the courtroom," boomed the Clerk's voice over the PA system, rudely returning Stanley to the real world.

The peremptory challenges moved quickly. Juror 2512, Juror 2436, Juror 2487, Juror 2523 — were all swiftly sent packing.

"Okay, people," the Commissioner testily admonished the lawyers when the proceedings stalled over the selection of the final juror. "You've each got one peremptory challenge left. So don't blow it. Now, get up here, Juror 2634 — and make it snappy."

Juror 2634, a surly young man wearing washed-out blue jeans and a tattered tee-shirt, sauntered to the front of the room. He flashed a peace sign to the Commissioner, then entered the box, taking the seat next to Stanley.

"Juror 2634, have you ever been charged with a crime?" the Commissioner asked.

"Sure," came the nonchalant response. "I got pinched once for shoplifting a Seven-Eleven. But the charges got dropped."

"Was there anything about that experience that would prevent you from deciding this case fairly?"

"Maybe. I got roughed up by the cops and jerked around by the prosecutor . . . ."

"Sidebar, your Honor," interrupted the City Attorney.

Commissioner Schwartz glowered at the young lawyer. "Forget it. I don't have time for sidebars. This guy stays. Now, Mr. City Attorney, do you want to exercise your remaining challenge?"

At that moment, the courtroom doors flung open. A bespectacled young woman burst into the chambers and ran over to the City Attorney, handing him a slip of paper. He read it, then shook his head in disgust.

"Well . . . ?" the Commissioner growled.

The youthful prosecutor stood up and looked at Stanley. "Yes, your Honor. The People ask the Court to thank and excuse . . . Juror 2281."

The land mine had detonated once again, this time with the force of an atom bomb. "Your Honor," Stanley suddenly blurted out, "a sidebar — *please*."

The Commissioner's eyes flashed angrily. "Juror 2281, are you deaf? Didn't you hear what I just told the City Attorney? Now, get back to the assembly room. And, by the way," he added as an after-thought, "thank you for your service."

~ ~

An ill-tempered jury supervisor greeted Stanley. "Well, 2281," he said with a smirk, "you've been dismissed from further service – at the special request of Judge Brown."

Stanley shrugged indifferently.

"You know," the supervisor continued, "I don't understand how you lawyers get away with it. I mean, always manipulating the system to your own advantage. One of the privileged few. There ougtta be a law . . . !"

Without a word, Stanley handed in his now tattered identification badge and walked away. On his way out, he passed the courtroom of Commissioner Schwartz, just as the City Attorney was coming down the hallway.

"Oh, Mr. City Attorney, a question please . . . ."

The startled prosecutor veered away, as if to avoid contact with the carrier of a dread disease. "I'm sorry, sir, but we're not allowed to speak to prospective jurors . . . ."

"I'm no longer a prospective juror," Stanley replied, "if I ever was one, that is. See – no badge."

"Okay, what can I do for you?" the City Attorney sighed, glancing impatiently at his watch.

"I want to know why you bounced me from the jury."

The young man laughed. "Oh, that's easy. You're a lawyer. It's our policy never to permit a lawyer to serve on a panel if it can be avoided."

Stanley was stunned. "Even if you have to take someone once charged with the very same crime over me?"

"My friend," the City Attorney answered condescendingly, "we'd take Jack the Ripper over you. It's the way our system works. But someone in your position should at least know that!"

As the young man started to walk away, Stanley caught him by the arm. "But how did you know I was a lawyer? The judge didn't ask me. What gave me away."

The prosecutor smiled slyly. "What gave you away, my friend, was the book I saw you carry out of the courtroom during the recess — *The Runaway Jury*. I figured you for a corporate lawyer. Only a corporate lawyer would think he'd learn something about jury service by reading John Grisham. While you were outside, I phoned back to my office and had them check you out with the State Bar. It was a close call, but we caught you in time!"

After the prosecutor had gone, Stanley called Katherine.

"I'm going back to the office, dear," he said wearily. "And tomorrow I'll be playing golf with Judge Brown."

There was a pause. "I take it you weren't chosen to be a juror, then, Stanley."

"No . . . no, I didn't have the privilege of serving," he sighed. "It seems the system can function without me."

SHARE AND SHARE ALIKE

Stanley Whitehead sat at the head of the conference table, his head in his hands, listening to his partners drone on about finances. Years before, when he'd donned the mantle of Senior Partner, Management Committee meetings had seemed—well—more meaningful, devoted to important cases being handled by the firm, recent developments in the law, the progress of associates toward partnership and how Whitehead & Williams could better serve its clients. Now, there seemed to be but one agenda item at every meeting—the Bottom Line. And, on this dreary November morning, as profits once again took center stage at the regular weekly gathering of the firm elite, Stanley found it impossible to suppress a yawn.

"And in conclusion, ladies and gentlemen," intoned Stephan Wise, the gaunt Vice Chairman, like a prosecutor summing up the evidence of a defendant's guilt, "the Finance Committee believes that, given the current economic climate, expense reduction is essential to our partnership's financial health. It's high time we did a little belt-tightening around here. And—as the first step—we recommend the implementation of a secretarial sharing program!"

Stanley sat bolt upright, as if a fire alarm had just sounded in the office. "*A what?*"

All eyes turned toward the Senior Partner, like those of rubbernecking spectators at the scene of a four-car pile-up.

"A secretarial sharing program," Wise repeated. "You know, partners sharing their secretaries with younger lawyers. Every other firm in town does it."

"But . . . why . . . ?" Stanley sputtered.

"To save money, of course. Look, Stanley, permitting partners to have their own secretaries is as outdated as carbon paper and three-cent stamps—a throwback to the days before personal computers, touch-tone phones and fax machines. Today, with sophisticated word processing programs, computer data bases and e-mail, a secretary can accomplish in ten minutes what it used to take an hour to do. Our proposal will produce substantial savings, all flowing to the Bottom Line."

Stanley cringed. There it was again—the Bottom Line. The Senior Partner was beginning to feel like a POW undergoing enemy indoctrination. It wasn't that he opposed change. He was a bit old-fashioned, maybe, but not reactionary. It was just that certain things were sacred . . . .

"I hear you, Stephen," he finally responded. "But surely there would have to be exceptions. For example, Doris Jones and I have been a team for more than twenty years. Bringing in another lawyer would be a terrible blow to the woman's morale . . . ."

Wise shook his head emphatically. "Stanley, there can be no exceptions. In fact, as the firm's leader, we would expect you to be the first partner to embrace the new program—to set an example for others. It's what your father would do were he alive today."

Oh, Lord have mercy, Stanley thought. There they go again! Whenever his partners wanted to rope him into something new, they unearthed the old man. Stanley turned and gazed at the portrait of the firm's founder hanging on the wall behind him, as if beseeching the stern-looking figure to intervene on his behalf. Then he remembered what his father had always counseled.

"Son, if you can't beat 'em, join 'em!"

"Stanley, you'll just have to learn to cope with change," Wise added.

The Senior Partner, sighing deeply, threw up his hands in surrender. "Whatever," he muttered. The issue had been decided.

~ ~

Around Whitehead & Williams, Thomas P. Tuttle was known as the Whirling Dervish. The young lawyer — now in his fifth year of practice — had the reputation of being the firm's most dedicated, hard-working and productive attorney, a legal dynamo. And it was to Thomas Tuttle that the Management Committee turned to share Doris Jones with Stanley Whitehead.

"Now, Tuttle," Stanley warned the young associate after he'd moved into a nearby office, "I want you to understand the close relationship that Miss Jones and I have shared over the years."

"Yes, sir," replied the dark, sparkplug of a lawyer, fidgeting in an oversized sofa chair in Stanley's corner office, glancing nervously at his watch.

"The woman is very sensitive about her position. You must treat her with the respect due someone of her status. In other words, you must always remember that *she is the secretary to the Senior Partner.*"

"Yes, of course," Tuttle said distractedly, leaning forward as if about to leave. "Now, is that all you wanted, sir?"

"And another thing," Stanley continued, ignoring Tuttle's not-so-subtle gesture. "You mustn't overwork her, taxing her with minutiae, burdening her with mundane and routine tasks."

"Yes, yes. Anything else, sir?"

The Senior Partner stood up and grasped the lapels of his jacket, like an evangelist addressing a gathering of the faithful.

"Of course, I'm not thinking of myself. I'm solely concerned with the welfare of someone I've become very attached to . . . . "

When the lecture was over, Tuttle bolted out of the office like an escaped convict taking leave of a floodlit prison yard.

Doris Jones waxed philosophical about the matter. "I understand completely, sir," the slim, silver-haired secretary told her boss when informed of the new arrangement. "In times like these, we all have to chip in and do our part. Besides, it should be interesting to . . . uh . . . er . . . get back into the mainstream of our practice."

Stanley regarded his secretary's professed attitude as stoic acceptance by a dedicated and loyal employee. After all, the woman had been his faithful assistant for more than two decades; she certainly wouldn't want to say anything to upset the boss to whom she was so devoted.

"Miss Jones," the Senior Partner called out to the secretary upon her arrival the next day, "Mrs. Whitehead and I would appreciate your addressing and mailing our Christmas cards again this year. You've always been so efficient at it."

The secretary grimaced as Stanley emerged from his office and emptied a shopping bag full of greeting cards onto her desk like a garbage collector unloading trash from a dumpster.

"I'm sorry, Mr. Whitehead," the secretary replied, "but Mr. Tuttle has me typing a big contract for Amalgamated Industries. He says it's critical that we get it out by the end of the day."

Stanley frowned. "But what about my Christmas cards?"

"Don't worry, sir. Your cards will be a perfect project for the trainees in the Word Processing Department. Of course, you'll have to help them with the names and addresses, and check that the right cards have been placed in the right envelopes . . . ."

"Never mind," the Senior Partner sighed, reaching over the top of her carrel and scooping up the cards like a rebuffed door-to-door salesman retrieving samples of his wares.

Several days later, returning from lunch, Stanley discovered a mountain of cardboard boxes, overflowing with documents, lying on the floor of his office.

"Miss Jones," he brayed over the intercom, "where did these boxes come from?"

"They're documents on the Anderson incorporation that Bill Poindexter left behind when he . . . er . . . departed the firm. Since you were the only other lawyer on the matter, the Records Department sent them up to you to make sure they're all marked correctly for our files."

Stanley cleared his throat. "But Bill Poindexter was so disorganized—that's why we fired him. Those papers are probably a mess. Plus, I don't know anything about filing documents! You've always done that for me."

There was a pause. "Miss Jones, don't tell me Mr. Tuttle has got you tied up again."

"Well, to tell you the truth, he does. We're trying to get out the merger agreement on the Consolidated/United matter, and then we have to turn to the closing papers on the Warwick financing. And with all the phone calls and people dropping by . . . ."

"When can you get to it?"

"Oh, maybe sometime next week . . . . But, really, this is an ideal job for a paralegal! I'm sure I can get one to help out — under your watchful eye, of course."

Stanley's silence was his consent.

Over the course of the next several weeks, Stanley saw very little of the secretary. When she wasn't frantically answering Tuttle's endlessly-ringing phone, rushing to the Mail Room or Messenger Department with envelopes marked "DELIVER ASAP" or "URGENT," or typing seventy-five words a minute on her desktop, she seemed to be in the associate's cluttered office taking dictation, organizing the piles of legal materials that littered his desk or simply lending moral support to the harried young lawyer.

One day, sitting alone in his office, fumbling with his personal computer, struggling to figure out how to use the firm's new e-mail system, Stanley decided to try an act of kindness to get his secretary's attention.

"Oh, Miss Jones," he called out as he saw her scampering to her desk grasping a stack of papers precariously in her arms.

The secretary, barely able to maintain her balance, stuck her head in the door. "Yes, Mr. Whitehead?"

"Miss Jones, I've been thinking. It's the holiday season, and I feel a bit like Ebenezer Scrooge. I'd like to take you to my club for lunch today and, after that, you can have the rest of the afternoon off for Christmas shopping . . . ."

"Oh, that's very kind of you, sir, but Mr. Tuttle has already invited me to have lunch at Burger King. After that, we'll be working the rest of the day catching up on correspondence. We're so busy—it's just like the days when you were a uh...er...a more active lawyer. But it was a nice thought. Maybe next year."

Stanley removed his half-moon glasses and rubbed his eyes wearily. "I should have known better," he mumbled.

It had at last dawned on the Senior Partner that his once-devoted secretary was experiencing no more difficulty adapting to the "mainstream" of the firm's practice than a child has in coming to terms with a hot fudge sundae. In fact, she seemed to be thriving on the overload of work to which she was subjected by Thomas Tuttle, actually preferring toiling for a lowly associate to handling the high-level affairs of the head of the firm. It was positively unnatural! Stanley thought. Contrary to the proper order of things.

The Senior Partner returned to the office after the Christmas holiday determined to remedy the situation.

"Tuttle," he greeted the young lawyer one morning, dropping into his office uninvited and unannounced. "I've just been reviewing our personnel records and have come across a most disturbing item. They show you've taken only eight vacation days in five years. You have almost four months of unused vacation time."

The young man smiled sheepishly. "I'm not sure what it is, sir. But I've always been so busy that I've never had the time...."

"Nonsense, Tuttle! By failing to take regular vacations, you've done a disservice to yourself, to the firm and to our clients. Vacations are essential to good physical and mental health. Accordingly—as Senior Partner—I order you to take all the time you have coming—immediately!"

The associate dropped his pen on his desk. "But Mr. Whitehead, I can't just disappear for five months. I've got a million and one responsibilities around here . . . ."

"Just find someone else to handle them," Stanley curtly interrupted. "Our lawyers are always willing to help each other out. We're all part of a team."

Tuttle sighed deeply, then shrugged. "I understand, sir. You're the boss. But you might want to reconsider . . . particularly in light of all the problems my absence would cause you."

Stanley cast a puzzled look at the young lawyer. "Problems? Me? What problems?"

The associate leaned back in his chair, put his feet up on his desk and placed his hands behind his head, a sly smile on his face.

"Yes, sir. You see, I've been assigned to handle the Universal Industries reorganization. John Treadway is the partner in charge, but he's on sabbatical right now and . . . well, if I'm off on vacation, that'll mean that you, as the relationship partner for the client, will have to handle the matter on your own . . . ."

"Never mind," Stanley muttered as he skulked out the door.

Stanley was discovering that separating Thomas Tuttle from Doris Jones was as daunting a task as dislodging a nasty cinder from his eye. The Senior Partner tried various schemes: a suggestion that the firm create an "executive suite" on his floor for Management Committee members only; a recommendation that associates be "rotated" to different offices every month so that individual attorneys could get to know each other better; and a proposal that Tuttle's office be converted into a storage room. All failed of adoption by the relevant committees of the firm.

"Give it up, Stanley," Stephen Wise finally counseled. "You're stuck with the guy."

One evening, wandering the corridors of Whitehead & Williams pondering his dilemma, Stanley came upon the portrait of his father that adorned the reception area, greeting all who entered the portals of the firm. As he looked up at the oil painting, a bewildered look crossed his face.

"Tell me what I should do, Dad," he addressed the wooden figure before him. "You always got your way around here. You had respect—influence. Me, they treat like a servant, a hired hand. We've got to do everything by committee now! The world is upside down—standing on its head. It's just not fair!"

Suddenly, Stanley thought he saw the old man shaking his head like a wise tribal elder. *"Remember what I told you, son,"* he seemed to be saying. *"Remember what I told you!"*

~ ~

"Mr. Whitehead, what's this all about?" asked Doris Jones, wide-eyed, as she arrived at her desk the following Monday morning.

A small crowd had gathered in front of Thomas Tuttle's office. Red, white and blue bunting wreathed his door; overhead hung a hand-lettered cardboard sign proclaiming "CONGRATULATIONS, TOM—WELCOME TO THE CLUB!"

"Go in and congratulate Mr. Tuttle," replied the lawyer, grinning. "He's the newest Member of the Firm!"

The secretary's jaw dropped. "Mr. Tuttle—a partner? But how . . . ?"

"We had a special partners meeting over the weekend. It was the decided that, despite the economic downturn, and the fact that he's only been with us for a short while—er, relatively speaking—young Tuttle has demonstrated extraordinary abilities and should be offered the brass ring. And it's a well-deserved honor."

Miss Jones was ecstatic. "Imagine—now I'll be working for two partners . . . ."

The Senior Partner smiled sadly, then put his arm around the secretary's shoulders. "I'm afraid not, Miss Jones. Mr. Tuttle will be moving—sooner, rather than later, I hope—to one of the junior partner's offices downstairs. And we have a strict rule that partners must share their secretaries with associates. So, from now on, you'll be working for Deborah Klutz—you know, the Trust and Estates lawyer."

"Ms. Klutz? Why, she only works part time, and does most of her work at home! Can't you make an exception to the rule for Mr. Tuttle?"

Stanley shook his head like a father comforting a small child after putting down the family dog. "Miss Jones, *there can be no exceptions*. The Management Committee wouldn't stand for it. No, you'll just have to learn to cope with change."The secretary frowned. "Besides," added the Senior Partner, "making Mr. Tuttle a partner will be good for morale. Yes, indeed—very good for morale."

THE BEASTS AND THE CHILDREN

"Oh, Dad, don't be such an old fogy!" chided Melissa Whitehead, standing before her father's cluttered desk, her arms folded, impatiently tapping her foot on the thick pile carpeting, looking like a frustrated mother confronting an obstinate child. "Just play along. It should be fun."

As the slim young brunette, dressed in a conservative gray suit and brown pumps, lectured the Senior Partner about his negative attitude, Stanley Whitehead—silently cursing the Management Committee for inflicting this godawful event on him—sat in his swivel chair, his elbows on his desk, his eyes down, staring blankly at a memo entitled "Take Your Child to Work Day."

"I'm not an old fogy!" he insisted, scribbling his initials on the document and tossing it into his Out Box. "I'm just skeptical—as any good lawyer would be under the circumstances."

"Dad, there's a difference between being a skeptic and being a wet blanket . . . ."

"And if I'm such an old fogy," Stanley huffed, ignoring his daughter's gentle jibe, "why did the Management Committee get me involved in the first place? I'm sure another partner would have served their purpose just as well . . . ."

"Dad, you're the head of the firm. Anyway, this is a terrific PR opportunity for Whitehead & Williams—good publicity about helping out kids, supporting the youth of our community—all that rah-rah sort of stuff . . . ."

"My, my! Who's being the cynic now?"

"Okay, okay, you got me, Dad. I'm a hypocrite! But you've always been so proud of the firm. I would have thought you'd be delighted to tell the children all about it. I wish you'd held something like this when I was growing up. If I'd known just how stodgy and stuffy this place was, I might never have come to work here!"

Stanley glared at his daughter, uncertain whether to treat her as an impertinent young lawyer or an errant offspring.

"Enough, already. I'll do it."

Melissa smiled coyly. "You sound nervous, Dad. You aren't worried our young guests might ask embarrassing questions, are you?"

"Nonsense! If I can deal with the juvenile antics of our Management Committee, surely I can handle a bunch of kids."

"That's the spirit. Now, shall we be off?"

"Yes, let's not be late for our important guests," Stanley replied half-heartedly, lifting himself from his desk and lumbering to the door.

"And," he added, an affectionate grin crossing his face, "I do want to thank you for helping organize this event. I knew there was a good reason why we hired you!"

When they arrived in the conference room, the two were greeted by a sea of children seated around a gigantic mahogany table. Over thirty in number, all were dressed up for the occasion, the girls in brightly-colored dresses, knee-length socks and shiny new shoes, the boys in newly-pressed jackets and conservative solid shirts and ties. Ranging in age from six to twelve, most sat quietly in their oversized leather chairs like Sunday school students awaiting instruction in the catechism.

"See, Dad," Melissa whispered to her father. "There's nothing to worry about. They're very well-behaved."

"We'll see about that," Stanley replied gruffly. "But tell me, why do their ID badges only show first names?"

"Because we promised the staff that the children wouldn't have to identify their parents. The firm doesn't want to put undue pressure on the youngsters."

Just then, a commotion arose in the back of the room. Stanley looked up to see a thin, hatchet-faced young man, dressed in a checkered sports jacket and faded blue jeans, a pencil stuck behind his ear and a small pocket notebook in his hand, stumble through the door. Slung awkwardly over his shoulder were a camera and a portable tape recorder.

"Sorry I'm late," the young man sputtered, smiling sheepishly as he wended his way to a table in the corner.

"Melissa, who the devil . . . ?"

The young woman grinned. "That's Tom Bennett, Dad. He's a reporter for the *River City Times*. They're doing a feature article on Take Your Child to Work Day. We told them they were welcome to cover our activities."

Stanley grimaced. "A reporter! I should have known . . . ."

After welcoming remarks by Melissa, Stanley launched into a rambling presentation on the history and traditions of Whitehead & Williams, attorneys-at-law. While his daughter operated a slide projector, the Senior Partner, reading woodenly from a prepared text, outlined the founding of the firm by his father nearly fifty years before, its growth from a struggling three-man shop to a regional legal powerhouse with over one hundred lawyers, its participation in major business deals and lawsuits over the years, its community and public service activities, and the like.

Midway through the presentation, as his diminutive audience stared bleary-eyed at the projector screen in stony silence, showing all the enthusiasm of schoolchildren forced to endure a lecture on proper oral hygiene, there appeared a slide entitled "Our Enlightened Workplace Philosophy." Showing a group of beaming young men and women of all sizes, shapes and colors, one in a wheelchair, the slide proclaimed:

> "Whitehead & Williams is more than simply an equal opportunity employer. The firm is a leader in fostering diversity in the workplace. Today, we boast a professional staff that is as broad-based as our society itself . . . ."

Before Stanley could say a word, small titters of laughter floated from the audience like gas bubbles escaping a bottle of carbonated soda. Suddenly, a tiny hand—attached to a dimpled girl with a blond pony tail—shot up. "Mr. Whitehead," she cried out, waving her arm in the air. "I have a question."

The girl, identifying herself as "Sally," stood up. Her eyes had the gleam of a hungry child who has just spotted an ice cream cone within easy reach.

"Mr. Whitehead," she asked, "is it true that, of your thirty partners, only one is a woman?"

Stanley froze. He grasped the back of a chair to steady himself, as if an unexpected wind gust had swept through the room. "Uh . . . er . . . ."

"It's true, Sally," Melissa Whitehead interjected, "that the firm has only one woman partner. But this reflects the historical difficulties that business law firms like ours have had recruiting qualified women from top schools, many of whom believe, quite incorrectly, that old-line firms are bastions of male chauvinism. But this trend is being reversed. After all, I'm a woman, and I was hired here!"

Stanley smiled benevolently at his daughter. "Thank you, dear—I mean, Ms. Whitehead. I couldn't have put it better myself. Now, moving on . . . ."

Another hand waved in the air, this of a blond-haired boy named "Jimmy," who bore a striking resemblance to little Sally. "A follow-up question, sir. Isn't it true that, at your firm, career advancement is more a matter of who you know than how talented you are? For example, isn't that why Ms. Whitehead was hired as a lawyer here? And aren't you Chairman just because your father founded the firm, even though today other lawyers bring in all the business and handle all the work?"

"Oh, Jimmy," countered a nonplused Melissa Whitehead, "nothing could be further from the truth. We're a meritocracy. I wouldn't be here today unless I had met the firm's strict hiring standards. And Dad—uh, Mr. Whitehead—wouldn't be where he is today unless he had demonstrated outstanding abilities in the legal world."

By this time, Stanley might just as well have fed his prepared presentation into a shredding machine. Eager little hands shot up around the table and, while reporter Bennett rolled his tape recorder, snapped photographs and scribbled notes, Melissa (with an occasional assist from her father) deftly fielded questions about maternity and paternity leave, day care, part-time employment, domestic partner health coverage and every other workplace issue confronting a large metropolitan law firm.

When the session mercifully ended, a relieved Senior Partner thanked everyone and shot out of the room with the alacrity of a hit-and-run driver departing the scene of an accident.

~ ~

While Melissa led the children on an informal walking tour of the firm, Stanley holed up in his office, behind closed doors, brooding. He knew this event had been a mistake: public relations gimmicks always were.

Just before noon, there was a delicate knock on the door. Opening it cautiously, Stanley found himself suddenly confronted by the collective horde, gathered about Melissa like munchkins around the Good Witch Glinda.

"And this is Mr. Whitehead's office," she announced with the practiced enthusiasm of a Disneyland tour guide. "Notice that it is twice as large as any other office. It shows what can be achieved through hard work and dedication!"

A Bronx cheer greeted this statement. Looking around, Stanley spotted Sally and Jimmy grinning at him maliciously from the back of the group.

Once she had deposited the children in the cafeteria for lunch, Melissa returned to check in with her father.

"Was that slide about being socially-conscious your idea?" Stanley asked testily.

"Dad, I was just trying to be relevant. These things are important to children nowadays. Besides, how was I to know these kids were so smart?"

Stanley shrugged. "I have to admit they're bright little tykes. Perhaps I've judged them too harshly . . . ."

At that moment, an ashen-faced messenger burst into the office. "Oh, Mr. Whitehead, I'm glad I found you," he said in a nervous, high-pitched voice. "You'd better get down to the cafeteria. Someone called 911 . . . ."

Without asking questions, the Senior Partner and his daughter pushed past the young man and flew down the hall to the cafeteria. There, they encountered three burly firemen, all clad in firefighting gear, one bent over a child lying face-up on the floor, holding her stomach and moaning.

"That's the man! That's the man!" came a shrill voice! "He's the one who did this."

"Seems like this little girl drank some sour milk," one of the firemen barked at Stanley, "but she'll be okay."

Another fireman produced a small plastic carton for the Senior Partner's inspection. "This one's a week past its freshness date. I guess you guys don't serve much milk around here."

"That's the man! That's the man!" came a shrill voice. "He's the one who did this."

Stanley looked up to see Sally dragging a scowling police officer by the arm, pointing in his direction. With them was Tom Bennett, holding a microphone in the little girl's face.

"Oh, Sally," Melissa exclaimed, placing herself between the child and the Senior Partner. "This was an accident, that's all."

The officer approached Stanley. "It may have been an accident, but serving stale milk to kids is against the law."

"Uh . . . er . . ." was all Stanley could muster in response.

"Mr. Whitehead," Tom Bennett shouted out, thrusting the microphone in Stanley's face. "Do you have any comment?"

"Uh . . . er . . . ."

The lawyer was rescued by the office manager, who entered the fray to arrange for the care of the stricken youngster, to accept a citation from the police and to utter a terse "no comment" to the reporter's questions. The shaken Stanley stumbled back to his office on his daughter's arm.

~ ~

"Melissa," Stanley grunted as the two sat in his office waiting for the lights to come back on, "I demand to know who those kids are!"

The stubborn associate shook her head emphatically. "No, Dad, I'm sworn to secrecy. My lips are sealed!"

"Those two are a menace. I mean, shutting down our electric power supply. Our offices are a shambles . . . the phones are ringing off the hook . . . ."

Just then, the office filled with light. "Thank God," the Senior Partner exclaimed.

"Oh, Dad, you can't fault the curiosity of an innocent child. Dave Collins probably thought there wasn't any problem letting Jimmy look at the control panel. Besides, kids are naturally mischievous. Don't you remember when I was ten, and stole the lipstick and mascara from the drug store?"

Stanley chuckled nostalgically. "Well, you weren't much of a thief — or, for that matter, much of a liar. I mean, with all that make-up on, you didn't exactly conceal your crime. But where are the children now?"

"They're in with Ruth Liman. She's explaining our corporate merger practice."

The Senior Partner blanched.

"I hope she isn't giving out any confidential information, particularly with that reporter skulking around!"

"Dad, you're getting paranoid," Melissa replied, gently patting him on the wrist. "But I'll look in on them, if it makes you feel better." With that, she jumped from her chair and darted out of the room like a frantic housewife who's just remembered that she left something boiling on the stove.

Things remained quiet for the next hour, while Stanley periodically eyed his watch as if monitoring the countdown to a missile launch. Then, like an alarm clock issuing a wake-up call, his desktop began emitting a chiming sound. He turned and saw that he had an e-mail message from the Computer Services Department, addressed to "All Clients Worldwide."

EMBARGO FOR LATER RELEASE
RIVER CITY, [   ], 1999. Sundance Corporation today announced that it will be commencing a tender offer for any and all shares of Moonbeam Inc. at a price of $[   ] per share . . . .

Stanley's slumped in his chair. "Holy Jesus," he moaned, dropping the mouse onto the floor.

"Dad, what's the matter?" Melissa Whitehead asked as she entered the office and observed her father in a daze. She walked over to him and peered at the screen, then broke out laughing.

Stanley gazed at his daughter in amazement. "What's so funny? That draft press release just went out to hundreds of clients! We could be ruined!"

Melissa raised her hand to silence the babbling Senior Partner. "Dad, please let me explain.

"First, that isn't a real press release. It's just a form our mergers and acquisitions people use as a model. There is no Sundance; there is no Moonbeam.

"Second, the e-mail didn't go out to clients. After Don Pollard told me he planned to conduct a demonstration of our system, I asked him to block any transmissions to clients from his computer. I had this feeling — particularly after Sally asked Ruth a lot of questions about how we protect confidentiality — that she was going to try something. I asked Don to attach that press release to an e-mail just to see what she'd do. Sure enough, she grabbed the mouse and clicked on the 'Send' button!"

Stanley sat back up, a relieved look on his face. "I'm glad you think it's so funny. I nearly had a stroke!"

"I'm sorry, Dad," Melissa replied, taking her father's hand. "I guess things got a little crazy today. Anyway, I've just sent Sally and Jimmy home with their mother. And I've asked Ruth to handle the farewell session with the kids. I figured you'd be too upset to do it."

Stanley scowled. "Well, now are you going to tell me who is responsible for those two brats?"

Melissa scratched her chin thoughtfully. "Oh, I guess I can tell you now. They're Jill Kelly's kids."

"Jill Kelly? The associate we just passed over for partner? I thought she quit?"

"She did, but with two weeks's notice. Since today was her last day, we had to let Sally and Jimmy participate. My guess is they were her parting shot at the firm."

"Too bad we can't fire her!" Stanley said, breaking into a smile. "Anyway—as they say—all's well that ends well."

Suddenly, his smile evaporated as he recalled the presence of a Trojan Horse on the premises. "Oh, my God," he exclaimed. "I forgot about that damn reporter. With everything he's seen and heard, he'll take us apart . . . ."

Just then, there was a rap on the door. A red-faced Tom Bennett stuck his head into the office.

"Oh, there you are, Ms. Whitehead. Well, I've searched everywhere for my notebook and my equipment, but I can't seem to find them. You're probably right: one of those kids must have swiped them when I went out to call my office. It's hard to believe how rotten children have become these days! It's our permissive society."

"How right you are, Tom," Melissa replied sympathetically.

"Anyway," the reporter continued, "it was sure nice of you folks to offer to replace the camera and the tape recorder. If the paper ever found out I'd lost them, I'd probably be fired!"

"Our pleasure, Tom," Melissa said. "We know how tough it is for a struggling young reporter like you."

"And, as we discussed, I'll return the favor by forgetting everything I saw today. I mean, why give any publicity to troublemakers like those kids? Just send over what you want me to say and I'll put it in the story."

"Thank you, Tom."

"No, thank *you*, Ms. Whitehead."

When the reporter had left, Stanley, shaking his head, turned to his daughter. "Melissa, you little devil! Tell me how you did it."

The young woman put a finger to her lips. "It's a secret. My lips are sealed! Let's just say I'm a more accomplished liar and thief than you thought."

"Fair enough. But we sure don't want a repeat of this debacle. We should begin planning for next year's Take Your Child to Work Day *now*. Don't you agree?"

"Next year?" she replied with a frown. "Dad, don't you think it would be better if we only did this—say—every other year? You know, give the PR machinery a rest...."

The Senior Partner smiled. "Very well, Melissa. But first I'll have to take it up with the Management Committee!"

THE REVOLVING DOOR

The following e-mails have been taken from the computer files of Whitehead & Williams, attorneys-at-law.

From: R. Stanley Whitehead, III (Doris Jones)
To: GW340.ADMIN.All Users
Date: 1/9/98 11:45 am
Re: Associate Departure

George A. Wilson will leave the Firm today. Beginning Monday, January 12, 1998, he may be reached at the Office of the State's Attorney, 180 Broadway, River City. Please join me at 4 pm in Conference Room 23C to bid farewell to George and wish him all the best. Refreshments will be served.
R. Stanley Whitehead, III
(By Doris Jones, His Secretary)

From: R. Stanley Whitehead, III (Doris Jones)
To: GW340.ADMIN.Management committee
Date: 1/12/98 10:12 am

Re: George Wilson

George Wilson dropped by late Friday afternoon to say good-bye. (I had completely forgotten about the farewell party.)
George said he was departing with the warmest of feelings toward the Firm. "The hardest part will be leaving those I've come to love and respect. After nine years, I feel like I'm walking out on a caring and nurturing family." I assured him—not without a touch of irony—that many of the partners felt the same way.

George also indicated that he completely understood the reasons he had not been made a partner this go-around. He admitted that his oft-cited failure to make a timely filing of motion papers (or whatever it was) in the Amalgamated anti-trust case (or was it the Rexford arbitration?) seven years ago—although of scant consequence at the time and never repeated—was sufficient to draw into question his reliability as a lawyer. I commiserated with the downtrodden young man, and expressed our disappointment that he had decided not to stick around yet another year to see if the brass ring would finally be his for the taking (he wasn't, after all, officially "turned over" at the time we rejected him for partnership). "Perhaps another year of seasoning, George," I said, "would have made a difference."

George mentioned, in passing, that his wife, Ellen, harbored some bitterness toward the Firm ("she thinks you guys really screwed me"). I responded that, knowing Ellen as I do, particularly the fondness and admiration for the partners she has always expressed to me, I was sure she would get over it.

R.S.W., III

(D.J.)

From: Doris Jones
To: R. Stanley Whitehead, III
Date: 1/12/98 11:24 am
Re: Departure of George Wilson

Attached is the form of e-mail message you dictated informing clients of Mr. Wilson's departure. (Sir, I know how you disapprove of my second-guessing you, but are you sure you want to keep the reference to "magic markers, paper clips and legal pads" in the e-mail? It seems rather disparaging of our hard-working young associates.)

144

D.J.
[ATTACHMENT]

WORK-IN-PROGRESS FILE

From: R. Stanley Whitehead<whiteheadrs
        @whitewillaw.com>
To: [Internet Address of Client]
Date: [Date]
Re: George Wilson

I understand that [name of partner] has informed you that George Wilson has recently left Whitehead & Williams. Although we value every member of our "family" of attorneys, no one is indispensable, and that is particularly true of associates, who are, in most cases, as interchangeable as magic markers, paper clips and legal pads. [Name of associate] has already taken over all of your matters from George. I'm sure that you will find the transition to be a smooth one.

[R. Stanley Whitehead, III, Chairman and Senior Partner]
[Stanley]
["Stinky"]

From: R. Stanley Whitehead, III (Doris Jones)
To: GW340.ADMIN.Partners/Retired Partners
Date: 6/6/98 4:45 pm
Re: George Wilson

I recommend to all partners the article in yesterday's *River City Times* entitled "Young Deputy State's Attorney Brings New Prosecutorial Zeal to Law Enforcement Agency." It seems that our recent alumnus, George Wilson, is making quite a name for himself in local law enforcement circles. Calling our former associate "the up-and-coming Thomas E. Dewey of River City," the article describes his unstinting efforts to crack down on organized crime, drug trafficking, gambling and prostitution in our community. It suggests that a shot at State Attorney General—or even Governor—may lie in George's future.

I put in a call to George to congratulate him on the favorable publicity. A paralegal returned my call, indicating that George was tied up on some sort of "hush-hush" investigation and unable to speak with me. Just like George—too wrapped up in his work to shoot the breeze with an old friend!

R.S.W., III

(D.J.)

To:	r. s. whitehead, iii
From:	reginald brickhouse
Date:	7/11/98 9:52 am
Re:	george wilson

i trust you noted the item in this morning's times about the new financial crime task force in the state's attorney's office. apparently, it's been formed to carry on the work of george's predecessor, tony angellini, who was recently disbarred for prosecutorial abuse and bribe-taking.

this sounds like trouble to me. as a former firm associate, george wilson knows a lot about our clients we wouldn't want getting around. i don't think he can be trusted.

rb

To:	R. Stanley Whitehead, III
From:	Doris Jones
Date:	7/11/98 1:30 pm
Caller:	Roberto J. Lopez (State's Attorney's Office)

[*] Telephoned   [ ] Please call
[ ] Will call again   [*] Returned your call
[ ] Wants to see you [ ] Came to see you
[ ] Urgent   [*] Left message
555-3401.

He was returning your call to George Wilson. ("Please stop harassing George with your constant phone calls. If you have questions about the Financial Crime Task Force, you should be talking to me, not George.")
D.J.

To: Reginald Brickhouse
From: R. Stanley Whitehead, III
Date: 7/11/98 3:42 pm
Re: george wilson — Reply

I telephoned George after receiving your e-mail. A secretary told me he would be out-of-pocket on a grand jury investigation all week and that she would have someone named Roberto J. Lopez call me back, which he did. I didn't return Lopez's call, but left another message for George instead.

I'm sure there is nothing to worry about, particularly with a level-headed, ethical fellow like George at the helm! Besides, our clients are all solid, law-abiding citizens who the state's attorney would have absolutely no interest in.
R.S.W., III

From: R. Stanley Whitehead, III (Doris Jones)
To: GW340.ADMIN.Management Committee
Date: 8/10/98 2:38 pm
Re: Indictment of Sidney Zeller

Reggie Brickhouse and I met earlier today with Roberto J. Lopez of the Financial Crime Task Force to discuss the indictment of Sidney Zeller of River City Realty recently handed down by the grand jury. We tried to meet with George Wilson, but were told that, due to ethical constraints, he had recused himself from the matter.

147

(George—who, as you may remember, worked for many years on the Zeller account while at the Firm—always was a stickler where ethics were concerned.)

We explained to Mr. Lopez that the prosecution of Mr. Zeller was without merit. Apart from his advanced age and obvious senility, I argued that Mr. Zeller could not possibly have known of the subsoil problem at Golden Age Estates before his company sold those luxury condos to local retirees. Mr. Lopez (a surly and thoroughly disagreeable fellow who speaks English like Desi Arnez) scoffed, noting that "we're out to get the economic elite of this town, and we're not about to listen to the lame excuses of some mouthpiece raking in $500 an hour." I can't recall ever having suffered such outrageous treatment at the hands of a so-called "servant" of the public. If I didn't know better, I'd say we and our clients were being subjected to some sort of "shake-down."

I am sure that George Wilson has nothing at all to do with this. This is obviously the brainchild of the State's Attorney, who is up for reelection this fall and would stand to gain politically by going after a prominent local businessman. Yet another reminder that politics is a dirty business—and how fortunate we are to be practicing a noble profession like the law!

R.S.W., III

(D.J.)

From:	R. Stanley Whitehead, III (Doris Jones)
To:	GW340.ADMIN.Management Committee
Date:	8/20/98 1:14 pm
Re:	Financial Crime Task Force

This morning, indictments were handed down against two more of our long-standing clients. Tom Dudley—

CEO of River City Financial—stands accused of fraudulently selling millions in worthless securities to the citizens of this community. (How could Tom—a director of the Boy Scout Council and prominent member of River City Presbyterian—have known that his brother was running a Ponzi scheme?) Ted Jessups—owner of River City Printing Co. and an old family friend—has been charged with illegal insider trading. (Ted assures me that, although his firm was handling the printing of the agreements for the deal, he didn't know of the pending merger of River City Industries and River City Enterprises when he purchased puts and calls on the stock of the companies just prior to the public announcement of the transaction. I, for one, believe him!) This brings to six the number of clients indicted since this task force of prosecutorial goons and thugs began its witch-hunt against the pillars of our business community. I have tried in vain to reach George Wilson, but, inexplicably, he hasn't returned any of my calls. (I did, however, receive a voice-mail message from that lout of an assistant of his, Roberto Lopez, accusing me of "stalking" George and demanding that I "cease and desist immediately before we bring you up on felony charges.") In the meantime, please rest assured that we will defend our clients vigorously.

R.S.W., III

(D.J.)

To:	R. Stanley Whitehead, III
From:	Doris Jones
Date:	8/20/98 4:32 pm
Caller:	Mr. Dudley (River City Financial)

[*] Telephoned   [ ] Please call
[ ] Will call again   [ ] Returned your call

[ ] Wants to see you   [ ]   Came to see you
[ ] Urgent   [*]   Left message

"What the hell is going on with this indictment? You guys told me everything I did was okay. Now they're coming after my wife and kids! Can't you get George Wilson to back off? I mean, he used to handle all our litigation! If you don't get this dismissed ASAP, I'm going to fire you and sue you for malpractice!"
Note to Mr. Whitehead: You also got a call from a young woman this afternoon. She didn't leave a message, but she sounded very much like Ellen Wilson. I can't imagine what she would want to talk to you about, but, knowing her as I do, I wouldn't let down my guard if I were you. She has a reputation of being a schemer and a conniving you-know-what. Just thought a word to the wise might be in order.
D.J.

PRIVATE AND CONFIDENTIAL

From: R. Stanley Whitehead, III
To: GW340.ADMIN.Management Committee
Date: 8/21/98 4:15 pm
Re: Ellen Wilson

George Wilson's wife, Ellen, called today. After exchanging customary pleasantries, Ellen asked me (apparently with reference to the recent indictments of six of our clients) "how it feels to be on the receiving end for a change." I told her that I would rather be undergoing a digital rectal exam. She then commented that "if the clients are going to the slammer, can their lawyers be far behind?"

Ellen added that George would be challenging the incumbent in this fall's State's Attorney's race. She said it had been a difficult decision for him because, although he had become a hero of the local media (they're now calling him "the Rudy Giuliani of River City") and the darling of the city's political big-wigs, "favorable press reports and stump speeches don't pay for the groceries." She also said — somewhat wistfully — that she imagined the only thing that could dissuade George from running for office would be a "meaningful" offer from a local law firm to take him in as a partner.

Playing along, I told Ellen that local firms generally do not admit to partnership someone who has demonstrated disloyalty by leaving the firm for another job without formally being terminated, although I confessed that many things had changed in the legal world in recent years. I suggested that, perhaps, a former associate could be admitted to firm membership if he could show that he was true partnership material and had overcome any earlier deficiencies perceived by the other partners. In the case of someone in George's position, it might be that some extraordinary act of public service would provide the necessary evidence.

We promised to stay in touch.

R.S.W., III

PRIVATE AND CONFIDENTIAL (EYES ONLY)

From:
 whiteheadrs<whiteheadrs@whitewillaw.com>
To: INTERNET: elliebabe@intrepid.net
Date: 8/22/98 3:12 pm
Re: Our Phone Conversation

This will confirm our earlier telephone conversation in which I told you that, although the compensation levels of partners at local law firms vary, those of George's background and experience are generally pulling down incomes in the $250,000 to $300,000 range. If you have any further questions, please let me know.
Stanley

To: R. Stanley Whitehead, III
From: Doris Jones
Date: 9/3/98   2:16 pm
From: Ellen Wilson

[*] Telephoned   [ ] Please call
[ ] Will call again   [ ] Returned your call
[ ] Wants to see you   [ ] Came to see you
[ ] Urgent   [*] Left message

"Everything has been arranged per our discussion!"
Note to Mr. Whitehead: Sir, what is going on? Have you been writing e-mails on your own without my knowledge? Is there some sort of trouble I don't know about? I don't like the looks of this one bit!
D.J.

From: R. Stanley Whitehead (Doris Jones)
To: GW340.ADMIN.Management Committee
Date: 9/7/98   4:58 pm
Re: Financial Crime Task Force

It is with great pleasure that I announce that the State's Attorney's office has dropped the charges pending against Sidney Zeller, Tom Dudley and Ted Jessups for insufficient evidence. Although indictments remain

outstanding against three other Firm clients, the new prosecutors assigned to the cases have indicated a willingness to accept plea bargains involving minor fines, community service and no jail time. I think we should send kudos to our litigation team—headed by the resourceful Reggie Brickhouse—for a job well done!
R.S.W., III
(D.J.)
P.S.   Ellen Wilson tells me that George has abandoned his plans to run for State's Attorney and will support the incumbent. I'm happy to see that the principles of loyalty we instilled in him while he was at the Firm have not been lost on our former associate.

> From: R. Stanley Whitehead, III (Doris Jones)
> To: GW340.ADMIN.All Users
> Date: 11/9/98 11:04 am
> Re: New Partner and New Associate

George A. Wilson returned to the Firm today as a partner, having resigned as Deputy State's Attorney after the reelection of the incumbent in Tuesday's elections. George brings with him a bright young colleague—Roberto J. Lopez—who will be joining us as a senior associate on a potential partnership track.

We welcome George back to the Whitehead & Williams family and congratulate him on his extraordinary acts of public service while a prosecutor. We also extend a warm "saludo" to Roberto. We hope to benefit—within the bounds of propriety, of course—from the inside knowledge of the workings of the State's Attorney's office offered by both of these able young men.

Please join me at 4 pm in Conference Room 23C to celebrate this happy event. Refreshments will be served.
R. Stanley Whitehead, III
(By Doris Jones, His Secretary)

To: R. Stanley Whitehead, III
From: Doris Jones
Date: 11/9/98 3:50 pm
Re: Left for the Day

I have left the office for a doctor's appointment. See you tomorrow.

P.S.   Don't forget the party at 4 pm—Conference Room 23C.

OTHER STORIES

PROHIBITION

Peter Donovan sat in his corner office, his jacket off, his feet propped up on his desk, savoring his afternoon cigar. As he launched perfectly-formed smoke rings into the air, then watched as they shimmered briefly in the bright overhead light before dissipating into a thin white haze, a contented smile crossed his face. The silvered-haired businessman felt an inner peace known only to the connoisseur of fine tobacco. For Peter, a cigar after lunch was a ritual as filled with meaning as singing the National Anthem before a ball game, watching a fireworks display on the Fourth of July or going to church on Christmas Eve: it centered him, provided meaning to his otherwise hectic existence.

Suddenly, there was a knock at the door. "Come in," he answered distractedly, as if in a trance.

Into the office strode a slim young woman dressed in a gray business suit, her auburn hair done up in a bun. Carrying a sheaf of papers bound with a thick rubber band, she approached Peter's desk and, placing her hands on her hips, glared at him like an angry mother confronting a wayward teenager.

Peter, awakened from his mid-day reverie, sat up with a start. "Cathy. What are you doing here?"

"Ah ha–caught you red-handed!" replied Cathy Donovan. "Maybe you ought to read these," she added, tossing the papers onto her father's desk.

Peter scooped up the documents, removed the rubber band and read with trepidation:

PETITION
WHEREAS, the River City Board of Supervisors has adopted Ordinance No. 98-78, entitled "A Law to Ban Smoking in Enclosed Places of Employment"; and

WHEREAS, the firm Peter J. Donovan & Associates, real estate brokers, is subject to said ordinance; and

WHEREAS, following the example of Peter J. Donovan, Chairman and CEO of said firm, many of the executives of said firm have continued to engage in the smoking of cigars, cigarettes and other tobacco products on the premises of said firm in blatant violation of said ordinance;

NOW, THEREFORE, the undersigned employees of the aforementioned Peter J. Donovan & Associates hereby petition, beseech, implore and demand said Peter J. Donovan to cease and desist, and to cause all executives of said firm to cease and desist, from so smoking cigars, cigarettes and other tobacco products on said premises, and to otherwise obey, and cause obedience to, the requirements of said ordinance.

The top petition bore the signature "Catherine E. Donovan, Attorney for Complainants." Underneath were some twenty counterparts signed by members of the office staff, including Peter's secretary.

Peter looked up in bewilderment. "Cathy, what is this?"

"Dad," she replied sternly, "it's a demand by your employees that you and your cronies obey the law. You know the anti-smoking ordinance has been on the books over six months now. Yet you continue to flaunt it by shamelessly puffing away in the office. Well, the staff is fed up with your behavior. And they've hired me as their attorney to make you clean up your act."

A soft smile suddenly crossed the young woman's face. "They thought I might have some influence with you," she added with a chuckle. "After all, Mom and I got you to stop smoking those foul-smelling stogies around the house."

158

Peter almost swallowed his Panatela. He had wondered whether it had been a good idea when his daughter, after graduating from law school, had decided to hang up her shingle as a sole practitioner in River City—in the same building as his real estate office, no less. But he'd never expected anything like this from his own flesh and blood. He cursed himself for having given her that biography of Sandra Day O'Connor for her fourteenth birthday.

"But you can't sue me, Cathy," he protested. "You're my daughter. It's . . . it's . . . unethical. Isn't it?"

The young woman laughed. "I'm not suing you, Dad. I'm just trying to reason with you. Besides, you're not going to make a *big stink* about this, are you?"

Peter cringed at this barb. "But . . . but . . . this is *my office—my firm*," he sputtered.

"I'm sorry, Dad. This may be your office and your firm. But the anti-smoking ordinance is *the law!*"

Peter glanced self-consciously at his smoldering cigar, then quickly dashed it out in the ashtray on his desk. He sank back in his chair and sighed. "My own daughter, handing me in to the smoking police. What next?"

Deep down, Peter knew he was fighting a losing battle. First, they'd banned him from airplanes, then from sporting events, then from restaurants and bars; now they were banning him from his own office. Since first reading about the city's latest foray against smokers, he had dreaded the coming of this day. But he was prepared–he had a plan. He wasn't about to be outsmarted by some neophyte lawyer–even if that lawyer was his own daughter.

"All we're asking, Dad," the young woman insisted, pointing toward the window, "is that you *take it outside!*"

Peter smiled slyly. "That's just what I intend to do, Cathy."

~ ~

The next day, returning from lunch, Catherine Donovan was confronted outside the building by a motley collection of men in shirt sleeves, seated on metal folding chairs around a circular aluminum table, sheltered from the elements by a giant patio umbrella, shrouded in smoke.

"Good afternoon, my dear," Peter greeted his daughter. "As you can see, we're following your suggestion. We've taken it outside."

He took a long drag on his cigar, then exhaled a foul-smelling cloud in her direction. "And I must say," he continued, emitting a phlegmy cough, "that smoking out-of-doors is a distinct improvement over smoking in the office. What with the sunshine, the fresh air . . . no phones ringing, no one barging in . . . ."

"But, Dad," she implored, fanning away billows of smoke, "you're subjecting everyone coming into and out of the building to noxious emissions. Besides, that table you've set up is blocking the entrance. It's a safety hazard."

Peter, confident of his legal position, shrugged nonchalantly. "That may be so, my dear, but we're in full compliance with the law. And isn't that what you wanted?"

The disgusted daughter shook her head and stalked away. "You haven't heard the last of this," she warned as she disappeared into the building.

The following afternoon, Peter's smoke fest was interrupted by an unsmiling young man in a red, brass-buttoned uniform.

"You gentlemen will have to vacate the area," he said after introducing himself as Lieutenant Christopher Dodge of Fire Company 109.

"But why?" Peter protested. "We're not violating the anti-smoking ordinance."

"No, sir, you're not," the Lieutenant replied politely. "But you are violating the city's Public Safety Code. You're blocking the ingress and egress to and from this building, creating a potential hazard in case of fire. You need a permit for that. Plus, if you gentlemen want to congregate regularly–and I assume you do–you'll need a separate public assembly permit. And, given current public opinion concerning smoking, I wouldn't count on getting those permits at any time before Hell freezes over."

As the youthful firefighter lectured the broker on his civic responsibilities, years of suppressed anger and resentment welled up inside him like rubbish backing up in a clogged sewer. He was tired of being treated as a public pariah, a social outcast, because of his beloved habit. It was political correctness run amok!

"Lieutenant, this isn't a police state. We're simply exercising our God-given rights as citizens . . . ."

The firefighter had apparently heard enough. "You may be correct, sir. If you want to sue the city, I'm sure the courts will be happy to resolve the matter–in, say, five or six years."

His face suddenly darkened. "But, in the meantime, I want you guys out of here–NOW!"

Wearing the forlorn expressions of toddlers just advised of the cancellation of a circus parade, Peter and his cohorts listlessly took down their umbrella, folded up their table and chairs, and extinguished their smoking materials in empty soda cans.

"Lieutenant," Peter asked as they were leaving. "How did you find out about us?"

"An anonymous tip, sir."

"From a woman?"

"I'm not at liberty to say. It's our policy never to disclose the identities of our informants."

~ ~

During the following weeks, Peter and his fellow smoking enthusiasts tried numerous schemes to enjoy their favorite mid-day pastime in peace.

First, they set up benches in the roofed walkway leading from the parking garage to the building, then puffed away as irritated pedestrians, casting venomous looks in their direction, passed by. This scheme was abandoned within a week when, one morning, Cathy barged into Peter's office and handed him an official-looking document entitled "Opinion of City Attorney on Application of Ordinance No. 98-78." The opinion stated, among other things, that "the term 'enclosed' in said Ordinance encompasses any structure with a floor and a ceiling, whether or not having walls. This would include, inter alia, covered pedestrian walkways . . . ."

"Hogwash!" Peter grunted. "That interpretation would never stand up in a court of law." However, not wishing to become a test case, the cautious business executive decided to comply.

Next, Peter and his friends, their giant umbrella in tow, moved their noontime festivities to the roof of the building, five stories above the street. Things went well for about a week, until several tenants complained of being pelted by ashes and smoldering cigar butts hurtling off the structure.

Peter agreed to use ashtrays, and to limit all smoking to the center of the tar and gravel roof, but his efforts came to naught when, one evening, a violent wind gust picked up the umbrella and sent it flying through a window of an adjacent building.

"You guys are a public nuisance," the building superintendent (a reformed smoker) railed at the executive the next morning. "My lawyer tells me I could have you evicted." Peter didn't bother to ask who the lawyer was.

"And if I catch you up there again," the manager warned, "I'm gonna lock all the exit doors and you'll have to jump off the building to get downstairs! Maybe that umbrella of yours will help break your fall."

Thwarted yet again, Peter commissioned an architect to study whether a balcony could be constructed outside his office to accommodate smoking.

"Well, Mr. Donovan," said the architect as he handed Peter a bill for $5,000 covering the preliminary work, "we could knock out your window and try to put in French doors leading onto a concrete balcony. But it'll cost you an arm and a leg, and, besides, on a windy day, you might get sucked out and blown onto the sidewalk before you had a chance to light up. Plus, the lawyers tell me you'll have to get a variance from the City Planning Commission to do it. Do you still want to go ahead with it?"

The lawyers again, thought Peter, as he showed the architect the door.

~ ~

Peter finally admitted defeat. "Cathy," he confessed to his daughter one day, dropping by her cluttered office on his way to a luncheon appointment, "I've given up trying to get around this anti-smoking law. From now on, I'm going to smoke my cigars on the sidewalk—like everybody else."

A relieved smile came to Catherine Donovan's face. "Oh, Dad, I'm so glad to hear it. I knew you'd eventually see the light."

"And, maybe—one of these days—I'll give up this nasty habit for good!"

"That would be great, Dad. You know Mom and I will support you."

Peter turned toward the door. "But first, I'm going to lunch . . . ."

A look of alarm came to the young woman's face. "But, Dad, before you go out, you should know . . . ."

Before she could finish her sentence, Peter had evaporated into the hallway.

An hour later, garbed in a yellow plastic raincoat, and carrying a small pink parasol, Cathy encountered her father maintaining a solitary vigil under the canopy of a curbside lunch wagon, his jacket collar turned up, his glasses befogged, soaking wet, a dead, half-smoked cigar dangling from his lips. She immediately rushed to his side, hoisting the parasol over his head.

"Oh, Dad," she said. "I was afraid you were going to get caught in this downpour. I tried to warn you about the weather before you went to lunch, but you left so quickly . . . ."

"Thank you, dear. But think nothing of it. It's the price we smokers have to pay. At least now no one can accuse me of violating the law!"

Cathy patted her father on the back like an understanding coach comforting a player after a losing game. "I'm sorry it had to come to this, Dad . . . ."

"It's not your fault," he replied, tossing the soggy cigar into the gutter. "You only did what you thought was right–exactly what I taught you to do when you were growing up. Now, let's get out of the rain!"

As the two walked arm-in-arm toward the lobby entrance, Peter felt a sudden blow on his backside. He turned to find a large man, dressed in an orange slicker, a billy-club in his hand and a menacing expression on his face, standing behind him.

"Hey, buster," the police officer bellowed, pointing toward the gutter, "just what is that?"

Peter's face turned ashen. "It's what's left of my cigar, officer," he replied shakily. "Don't tell me I'm violating the anti-smoking ordinance again . . . ."

The officer jammed the billy-club against Peter's chest. "You're not violating the smoking law, buddy – you're littering! I could cite you for that. But, I'll let you off with a warning this time. Now, go over there and pick that thing up."

The battle-weary real estate agent staggered over to the curb and retrieved the water-logged remnants of his cigar. "Uh, what should I do with it now, officer?" he asked, meekly holding it up to the policeman's face.

The cop glared at the errant smoker. "Get rid of it!" he barked. *"Take it inside!"*

With that, Peter and his daughter trudged back into the building to face a smoke-free world.

THE RIGHT PLACE

The young man stood before the open door, peering into the dimly-lit room, wondering whether to go inside. Like an awkward teenager at his first school dance, he shifted uneasily from one foot to the other, tugged at his shirt sleeves and straightened his tie. As he watched others enter, he had that same hollow feeling he always had in situations like this, the sensation of having gotten off the bus at the wrong stop. Maybe this group idea was a mistake, he thought. Maybe he should grapple with his personal demons on his own.

He tried to reassure himself. He shouldn't let baseless fears get in the way: after all, he'd been to places like this before, knew what went on there, knew what he had to say. And tonight he was prepared. He decided to go in.

As he stumbled through the door, a dark, chunky, spark-plug of a man approached him, his hand extended in greeting. "Hi, I'm Don," he said, pumping his visitor's arm mechanically.

The young man jumped, as if accosted by a mugger. "Uh . . . er . . . hello," he sputtered, "my name is Tyler. . . Tyler Tinker."

"Welcome," the man replied with a waxen smile. "You're in the right place."

Freeing himself from the stranger's grasp, the tall, gangly visitor bolted inside and scurried to the nearest corner. There, he breathed easier, like a soldier enjoying a brief respite from battle.

Although this was his first time here, the room had a familiar air. The gray cinder block walls, the ground glass windows, the flickering fluorescent lighting, the coffee table in the back and the metal folding chairs arranged in a circle on the scuffed linoleum floor reminded him of other meeting rooms he'd been to. The twenty or so others who'd gathered that evening, hovering in tightly-knit clusters of threes and fours, carrying on animated conversations, like guests at a cocktail party, also seemed familiar, although he knew no one in the room. Even the seemingly obligatory band of smokers, furtively puffing away near an open door in the rear, gave the place a comfortable and friendly atmosphere. He began to relax.

"TWO MINUTES," a disembodied voice boomed from the center of the room. "Let's wrap up the small talk, people."

Just then, a girl in a white blouse and short blue skirt approached the young man. "Hi, I'm Mary," she said in a soft, inviting voice. "You must be new."

He gawked as she held out her hand, transfixed by her doll-like features — her long blond hair, bright green eyes, high cheekbones, full, moist lips . . . .

"Oh, hello," he replied, his voice cracking. "I'm Tyler Tinker. And you're right — this is my first time."

The girl giggled. "I thought so. I can always tell the newcomers. They stand in the corner or against the wall, like they don't belong here."

The visitor blushed. "What I mean is, it's my first time *here* — at this particular meeting," he stammered. "I've been going to another group for about three months now, but came here tonight just for a change. Sometimes, you get a little tired of hearing the same old things over and over again."

"Isn't that the truth!" she answered, gently patting his arm. "But you'll like it here. Everyone is so nice. We aren't judgmental, like in other groups. Our motto is 'Live and let live.'"

168

The young man smiled. "I'm glad to hear that. The ego at these sessions can get pretty thick. Everyone trying to knock each other down. Sometimes you feel like you're in the middle of a barroom brawl!"

The girl nodded. "I know. It's so important to find a group that's supportive. I mean, why come if the people there don't encourage you, aren't sensitive to your feelings?"

As the young man gazed at the girl, imbibing her comforting words, he began to feel a warm glow rising within him, like the sensation, he thought, of sipping a glass of sherry.

"And another thing," she continued, as if reciting from a script, "there's genuine honesty in this room. No bs. I think people should be totally real at these meetings. Don't you agree?"

The young man hesitated, furrowing his brow pensively. "Well . . . I suppose so. But in this sort of free-spirited setting, a certain amount of artistic license is to be expected. It comes with the territory."

The girl gave him a puzzled look, then laughed. "I guess you're right. They say that people like us are basically insane."

"MEETING TIME, MEETING TIME!" boomed the mystery voice.

"Come on, let's sit together," said the girl, taking the young man by the hand and leading him to the circle of chairs. "I think you'll appreciate the unconditional love you feel in here," she said, squeezing his hand as they entered the small enclave.

Unconditional love! The words swirled in the young man's head like an intoxicant. He was in the right place.

As they took their seats, he leaned over and whispered in her ear. "Believe it or not, I was really nervous about coming tonight. I can't be too careful about where I'm seen. If my bosses ever found out I was going to a group like this, there'd be hell to pay. They'd think there was something wrong with me. But, after talking to you, I know I'm where I belong."

He reached into his jacket pocket and produced a small blue notebook.

"Are you planning to take notes?" the girl asked. "I've never seen that before."

"Oh no—it's my reading for tonight," he said, smiling. "I think I've got something really good this time."

She returned his besmitten look with a blank stare.

"Good evening," the voice said. "Welcome to the Westside High and Dry Forum. My name is Randy, and I'm an alcoholic."

The young man suddenly jumped to his feet. All eyes were upon him, like those of a jury about to deliver a verdict of guilty. He gazed down at the girl with the forlorn expression of a child who has just been told to go to his room. She gazed back, wide-eyed, as if suddenly confronted by an unwelcome intruder. Then, without saying a word, he sprinted toward the door and out into the hallway.

At the front entrance, he breathlessly questioned a security guard. "Pardon me, but I'm a bit lost. Could you tell me where I might find the meeting of the Westside Poetry Circle?"

The security guard smirked. "Two doors down and to your left—*to your left*—you can't miss it," he barked, as if he'd been asked the question before.

"Oh," the young man replied, as he looked back down the long, dark corridor, scratched his head and sighed.

THE BUSYBODY

Iris O'Reilly was never shy about intruding upon the privacy of her fellow workers. Whether cornering a group of secretaries huddled around the coffee machine, gossiping idly ("My, how birds of a feather do flock together!"), interrupting an impromptu gathering of clerks grousing about work in the employee lounge ("Talk about stumbling into the lion's den!") or confronting an assistant VP trying to sneak out early ("Who let you out of your cage, Henry?"), Iris, personal secretary to the President of the First National Bank, constantly butted in where she wasn't wanted. Even when she was at her desk, just off the lobby, typing some memo or letter for her boss, Iris's colleagues felt her watchful eyes upon them.

"She's always spying on us," they'd say when out of earshot. "Why doesn't she leave us alone?"

Yet, for all her seeming ubiquitousness, Iris remained largely a mystery to those around her. Widowed, living alone in a small one-bedroom apartment, the wispy, white-haired Iris never socialized with co-workers. Lunchtimes, she'd shun the cafeteria, choosing instead to leave the Bank, bulging handbag in tow, to disappear into the park across the street.

When, following a brief illness, Iris unexpectedly departed this world, there (along with the usual expressions of shock and grief) a general sense of relief that she'd no longer be around—watching.

Unfortunately, the feeling of well-being that followed upon Iris's demise was short-lived. No sooner had the secretary been laid to rest than Tom Foxx, the Bank's harried Assistant Controller, made a startling discovery rummaging through her desk for personal effects.

"I wonder what's in this?" he remarked to Chief Teller, Robin Fowler, holding up a bulky manila envelope, taped shut and provocatively labeled "I. O'Reilly—Photographic Evidence." "I found it in Iris's bottom drawer, along with an unused roll of film."

Robin, perched atop a stool behind her teller's window, uttered a muted squeak, then hopped away, as if Foxx held a hornets nest in his hand. "Uh . . . I'm not sure I want to know," she stammered.

"I'm not either," Tom replied.

Taking the envelope to the safety of an empty office, the two speculated as it its contents.

"I bet they're photographs of us—the staff," said the tall, red-headed Robin. "Taken in awkward or compromising situations—probably with a hidden camera. You know what a busybody Iris was. Constantly spying."

"You're probably right," agreed the thin, browned-haired Tom. "Who knows what she caught us doing around here."

Robin turned noticeably red. "Oh, my God! I wonder if she ever photographed me . . . ."

"Yes?"

"Never mind."

Tom's jaw suddenly dropped. "Gosh, maybe she caught me . . . ."

"Yes . . . ."

"None of your business."

Tom and Robin quickly agreed that Iris's photos could be explosive. They also agreed that, because the Bank was the executor of the deceased secretary's modest estate, they couldn't destroy the envelope without violating the law. They decided to hide it in a secure place while they figured out what to do with it. "Let's lock it in a safe deposit box," Tom volunteered. "No one will find it there."

"And we can't let anyone know we have it," said Robin. "Those photos could be used for blackmail — which I'm sure," she added haughtily, "is exactly what Iris intended them for."

Despite their vows of secrecy, word of the envelope (as well as of its presumed contents) soon spread through the Bank like a nasty virus. (Robin had told her friend, cashier Denise Breckenridge, who'd in turn informed all her colleagues, while Tom had told his assistant, Mike Angelo, who'd immediately passed it on to the entire administrative staff.)

"I'd just love to see those photographs," said Myra Donovan, the Bank's Property Manager, strolling uninvited into Tom's office one morning. "Naturally, I'm not concerned about myself. It's Sheila Jones I'm interested in. She's been pilfering office supplies. Maybe Iris caught her red-handed. As Assistant Controller, it's your job to find out!"

"Must be some interesting snapshots in there," suggested teller Tim Johnson while he and Tom stood in the cafeteria line later that day. "Of course, I'm sure there aren't any of me. But what about Pete Drysdale? He's been 'borrowing' from the cash drawer for years. Bad gambling habit, you know. Iris could have photographed him in the act. You better investigate!"

"I wonder who's in Iris's rogue's gallery," mused assistant loan officer Doris Wanamaker, confronting Tom as he emerged from the men's room's, preparing to leave for the day. "I'm certainly not in it, but I bet that little tramp, Betty Gunnerson, is. She's been carrying on with Horace Witherspoon like there's no tomorrow. Iris probably caught them together in the lounge or the vault. You should be concerned about our reputation!"

Despite the pressure, Tom steadfastly refused all requests to see the allegedly incriminating photos. "No one's getting their hands on that envelope," he vowed. "Not even the President. The seal will not be broken!"

To make certain the envelope was secure, Tom surreptitiously removed it from the safe deposit box and placed it in his office safe, where he could keep an eye on it.

~ ~

Tom hoped his stubborn refusal to let anyone see the photos would put an end to the matter. After a week enduring hostile stares and admonitions to "do your job," he noticed that office buzz about the envelope seemed to subside. Employees returned to their normal routines — sloughing off assignments, taking extended coffee breaks, gossiping behind one another's backs — habits that Iris had so detested. The flap over the photos appeared to be at an end.

Then, one morning, arriving early, Tom noticed his office door ajar. Peering in to investigate, he was stunned to discover, fluttering about in front of an open safe, none other than Robin Fowler. The Chief Teller, papers scattered about her, was distraught.

"Oh, Tom," she cried when she saw him walk in. "They're gone. Someone's taken them. We could be ruined!"

Angrily slamming his briefcase on his desk, Tom glared at the would-be burglar. "What are you doing here?" he barked. "And how did you get into the safe?"

Robin smiled meekly. "Uh . . . I kind of broke in this morning and found the combination in your top drawer . . . ."

"That still doesn't explain why you're *here* – *in my office!*"

"Er . . . I was trying to find Iris's envelope," Robin muttered. "You see, when you took it from the safe deposit box, I was sort of hiding behind the glass partition, watching. I saw you put it in here."

Tom scowled. "And just why were you trying to find the envelope?"

"I was afraid someone would get at the photographs before I . . . I could see what was in them. I wanted to find out if Iris ever caught me . . . I mean, any of the tellers — oh, you know how sometimes we sit behind a 'Next Teller Please' sign, reading a magazine or fixing our nails, while a long line of customers waits at another window . . . ."

Contrition suddenly turned to anger as Robin snapped at her co-conspirator. "How could you have been so stupid as to let someone steal them?"

Tom shook his head. "Aw, quit squawking, Robin. The photos are perfectly safe. Truth is, I got nervous myself and took them home with me last night. See, here's the envelope," he said, removing it from his briefcase. "Still sealed."

Robin breathed a sigh of relief. "Thank God. I've . . . we've been spared."

Grim-faced, Tom pounded his fist on his desk. "That does it," he growled. "I'm sick and tired of that damn envelope. I don't care if we are Iris's executors. I'm taking it over to Kinkos and shredding it!"

All eyes were upon the Assistant Controller as he stormed out of the Bank, the infamous envelope under his arm.

~ ~

Once outside, Tom encountered Jonas Dutton, the Bank President, on his way in to work. "If Iris were still around," Dutton chortled, elbowing Tom in the ribs, "there'd be hell to pay. She hated tardiness — particularly mine!"

Just then, Dutton noticed the envelope. "Oh, you've got Iris's photographs," he said. "I wondered what happened to them. I couldn't find them anywhere."

Tom, speechless, turned white.

"No matter," the portly President continued, retrieving a small package from his jacket pocket. "I just picked these up over at Photo-Mat. They called yesterday, asking for Iris. These are the last pictures she took before she died."

Opening the package before the shaken Assistant Controller, Dutton removed several glossy prints. "This must be the baby orangutan I read about in the papers," he chuckled, thrusting a photo in Tom's face. "And here's one of Rajah, the Bengal tiger. Been there since I was a kid."

Tom stared at the photos, his mouth agape. "Huh?'

Dutton waxed nostalgic. "Iris was quite the animal lover. Went to the zoo almost every day. She enjoyed watching her beloved creatures frolic and play."

"No . . . er . . . I didn't realize . . . ."

"Well, when the Parks Department budget was cut last year, she became concerned about deteriorating conditions — you know, overcrowding, poor sanitation, stuff like that. She started a campaign to raise private funds for the zoo. She wanted to show what was going on — to get folks to support her cause — so she started taking these photographs. The folks over at City Hall got pretty upset with her. Thought she was butting in where she didn't belong."

Dutton took the envelope from Tom, opened it and dropped the prints inside. "Why don't you go through these" he said, returning it to the employee. "Send any of interest over to the Humane Society. I'm sure that's what Iris would have wanted."

Trailing the President, a dazed-looking Tom Foxx stumbled back into the Bank, the open envelope in hand. Anxious faces followed him closely as he passed through the lobby. Suddenly, he had an idea.

"I'll look at these right away, sir," he called out as Dutton disappeared into his office. "And I'll be sure to let you know if I find anything interesting!" He smiled slyly at his fellow workers.

Since that day, Tom has been treated with the utmost respect at the Bank. The staff has nothing bad to say about him, even when he's not around-watching.

ROLE MODEL

Rush hours, you could usually find Bob Goodman, on his cell phone, cruising the streets of River City in his blue Chevy van. You might have spotted him approaching the Main Street off-ramp on Highway 5, where a stalled vehicle was blocking the right-hand lane; or at the corner of Fifth and Elm, where a traffic signal was on the blink; or skirting a line of orange cones on Central Avenue, where a pothole was under repair. And, if you happened to be tuned in to talk radio station WRIV – 1030 on your AM dial – you might have heard "Tipster Bob" himself reporting the traffic tie-up unfolding before you, live from the scene.

At sixty-two, Bob Goodman was River City's one and only radio traffic reporter, a role he'd undertaken after losing his job in public relations to a man twenty years his junior. Often finding himself mired in traffic jams as he looked for other work, the stocky, balding Bob began killing time between job interviews by phoning in reports on highway conditions to WRIV, describing snarls, snags and slowdowns, and suggesting alternate routes for motorists. His frustration quickly turned into a sense of accomplishment when the station started broadcasting the information, giving Bob on-air credit.

Unfortunately, he earned little more for his efforts than occasional kudos from the station. When his wife, Estelle – now the childless couple's sole breadwinner – complained that WRIV should be paying him for his tips, Bob broached the issue with the station's management.

"I'm sorry, Mr. Goodman," explained Tom Kelly, WRIV's boyish-looking General Manager, "but that would be out of the question. You provide us with news. And we never pay for news. It's a matter of policy."

When, however, Bob threatened to "reconsider this whole traffic tipster thing," Kelly softened his position.

"Of course, you *are* a loyal listener, and you mean well. And we wouldn't want to lose your services. Perhaps there's some way we can recognize your contribution . . . ."

That evening, Bob beamed triumphantly as he pulled into his driveway, sounding his horn to catch Estelle's attention. Emerging from the van, he gazed proudly at the makeshift sign now mounted on the roof:

SAY HELLO TO "TIPSTER BOB"
OFFICIAL TRAFFIC REPORTER
WRIV RADIO–AM 1030
"ALL TALK, ALL THE TIME"

"What have you done to our van?" cried Estelle as she ran out the kitchen door.

"Honey, you're looking at the WRIV Traffic-mobile! What do you think?"

Estelle stopped in her tracks. "I think you're crazy, that's what I think. Exactly how much are they paying you to be a traveling billboard?"

There was a prolonged pause. "Well . . . uh . . . er . . . nothing, really. But just look at this!" he added, excitedly handing her a document he scooped off the front seat. "It's a letter from the General Manager appointing me Official Traffic Reporter! They're even getting me a new cell phone and a set of vanity plates. They recognize the importance of getting my message out to the community!"

The slender, silver-haired Estelle stared at Bob in disbelief. "Message! What message?"

Bob smiled weakly. "Oh, you know," he stammered. "My message about being a good citizen—about helping others."

Estelle shook her head and sighed. "Bob, can't you see these people are just using you? Once they're through, they'll toss you out like yesterday's trash—like your old bosses did!"

With that, Estelle crumpled the letter into a ball and threw it at her startled husband. She turned and stalked back into the house.

~ ~

Convinced Estelle was overreacting, Bob was undeterred. He abandoned his job search and became a full-time traffic tipster, taking to the streets of River City daily, on the lookout for fender benders, jack-knifed big-rigs and other highway horrors. Now broadcast live from the Traffic-mobile, his insights on local travel conditions soon became a staple of WRIV's regular half-hourly news segments. With his background in public relations, Bob sprinkled his reports with homespun wit and wisdom ("Folks, it looks like an old mattress has fallen off a pick-up on the northbound 115. It's *bedlam* out there!"). In addition to his regular spots, listeners were treated to "Bob's Tip of the Day"—a prerecorded message from "Your old friend, Tipster Bob" urging motorists to "Drive Defensively," "Keep Your Eyes on the Road" or "Stay Alert and Stay Alive."

Now a recognizable celebrity, Bob began attracting attention around the small metropolis. Passing motorists would smile, wave and honk as they encountered the van. Traffic cops and meter maids would salute when Bob came into view. Children would gather around wherever he parked near a school or playground, begging to see the Traffic-mobile up close. One afternoon, an elderly woman with a flat flagged him down along a busy highway and asked if he'd be kind enough to call Triple-A for her.

"I normally don't trust strangers for help," she explained, "but when I saw the blue van and realized it was you, I didn't hesitate. You're practically family."

Bob rolled up his sleeves and changed the tire himself.

In fact, the traffic reporter quickly became a magnet for those in need of a good deed. A retirement home asked if he'd mind taking residents on occasional spins around town in the Traffic-mobile for sunshine and fresh air. He began running errands for charities, delivering meals to shut-ins, blood to hospitals and stray pets to their owners. Receiving several fan letters a day, he accepted invitations to speak before civic groups and school assemblies on subjects ranging from highway safety to community service. *The River City Times* even chose him "Citizen of the Month," celebrating his efforts in a piece entitled "More Than Just A Good Traffic Reporter—A Good Samaritan."

Bob's extensive extracurricular activities occasionally interfered with his official duties at WRIV. Soon, there was talk around the station of organizing a group of volunteer "senior citizen" traffic observers—to be called "The Gray Patrol"—who, under the direction of a newly-promoted "Captain Bob," would drive the streets of River City, phoning in traffic tips to supplement his reports. "Might be a good idea to widen your . . . uh . . . perspective, Bob," Kelly told him. "You know, expand your field of vision by having more volunteers like you watching out for traffic problems. It'd also be good PR for the station—show that we support the involvement of . . . uh . . . er . . . older folks like you in community affairs. Certainly couldn't hurt at license renewal time!"

"You see, honey," Bob crowed to Estelle one evening as he sat at the kitchen table, poring over a road map of River City preparing his next day's itinerary, "you were wrong. I am appreciated. People are getting the message!"

His wife shrugged. "Maybe so," she replied. "But all this hoopla reminds me of those silly press releases you used to write: it just seems too good to be true."

~ ~

Several days later, Bob was at River City Middle School, preparing to make a presentation on pedestrian traffic safety, when his cell phone rang. Just about to step onto the stage, he shut it off and went ahead with his half-hour talk. "Get the word out," he urged his young audience. "Safety is everybody's business!"

After he'd left the auditorium, a breathless school official ran up to him in the parking lot and handed him a phone message from Tom Kelly. "It sounded pretty important."

Bob jumped into the van and drove off. As he left the school grounds, he dialed Kelly back.

"Goodman, where have you been?" the irate General Manager growled through the static. "There's been a four-car pile-up on Highway 5. It's been backing up traffic for almost an hour. We don't have anyone else available to cover it."

"Well . . . um . . . I've been tied up . . . ."

"I don't care if you've been in intensive care. All I know is you're not doing your job. Now, get over to the scene — ASAP!"

Bob hung up, made a U-turn and started heading north. He hadn't gone more than a block when he heard a siren blaring and saw lights flashing behind him. A police car pulled him over to the curb.

"Sorry about the U-turn, officer," he said, "but I've got to get to the scene of an accident over on I-5. I'm Tipster Bob, you know!"

The officer smiled mechanically. "Mister, I don't care if you're the man in the moon. And I didn't pull you over for the U-turn. I stopped you for violating Ordinance 00-123 — illegal use of a cell phone while operating a motor vehicle. City Council passed it last week. Mobile phones have been responsible for a lot of accidents lately."

"I didn't know . . . . I mean, I've been so busy, I haven't been following the news."

The cop pulled out his ticket book. "License and registration, please," he said.

The WRIV brass, pulling a few strings in high places, managed to get the ticket fixed. Although this avoided publicity about the incident, the station nevertheless put the idea of "The Gray Patrol" on hold and placed Bob himself on an indefinite leave of absence.

"We hate to do this to you, Bob," Tom Kelly explained as the defrocked traffic reporter handed in his "TIPSTER1" license plates. "But, like it or not, you've become a role model around this town. And we can't have a role model ignoring traffic laws — particularly in a school safety zone. It just won't do."

"But I was only doing my job," Bob said plaintively. "Trying to be helpful."

"Besides," the General Manager continued, as if Bob had said nothing of any consequence, "what with the new cell phone ordinance, we're reconsidering this whole traffic tipster thing. We don't want to do anything that might encourage listeners to violate the law. Wouldn't be good for our image. And, anyway, there's a limit to how much someone in your . . . your *position* can do for us. Face it, Bob, you just aren't as useful as you once were."

Bob was appreciative that at least Estelle—who had every right to gloat—didn't harp on his downfall. "I'm sure you'll find something else," she said wistfully. "Somewhere."

But Bob, ever the optimist, was confident that one day he'd return to the streets of River City to broadcast his message. He remained hopeful until the morning when, awakened by a loud noise outside, he peered out his bedroom window and saw a banner proclaiming "SAY HELLO TO CAPTAIN JIM—WRIV-AM AERIAL TRAFFIC REPORTER" trailing from a helicopter hovering overhead. It was then he decided he'd better find another job—and, maybe, another message.

THE GRANDFATHER CLOCK

The grandfather clock chimed five, and the white-haired Chairman (Emeritus), fidgeting behind his aging wooden desk, prepared to leave for the day. It had been a slow afternoon — no mail, no phone calls, no visitors dropping by. Things were always quiet this time of year, he told himself.

There was a knock at the door. A sandy-haired young man stood in the hallway, awkwardly peering into the tiny office.

"Sorry to bother you, sir," the intruder said sheepishly. "But may I ask a question?"

The older man beamed. "Why, of course. Come right in Mr. . . . er . . . ."

"Finch, sir. Alan Finch. From Finance."

"Ah, yes — Finch — from Finance. I hope you had no trouble finding me," the Chairman said, pointing his visitor to a worn-out sofa chair. "When I stepped down last year, they gave me this little cubbyhole to conduct my personal business. Rather out-of the-way, don't you think?"

"I'll say," the young man replied, looking around the cramped, dimly-lit quarters. "I've never been on this floor before. With all the boxes and crates down here, it sort of looks like a storage shed."

"How can I help you?" the Chairman asked, feigning indifference to the young man's observation. "I never was very good at the numbers, but I hope I can be of assistance in some other way. I'm always interested in hearing from our . . . I mean, the firm's . . . professional staff. That's why I'm here — to provide young people like you with the benefit of my years of experience."

The visitor shifted uncomfortably in his seat. "Well, it's actually kind of embarrassing . . . ."

The Chairman smiled benevolently. "Let me guess. You feel overworked. Now, when I was a young fellow like you . . . ."

"No, sir. That's not the problem. I'm quite satisfied with my workload."

The older man scratched his head. "Oh, I know! You feel unappreciated — that the Firm has failed to recognize your contribution. Let me tell you the story of . . . ."

"That's not it, either. I'm told my work is outstanding."

The Chairman was undaunted. "Then the pressures of the job are putting a strain on your marriage. Your situation reminds me of . . . ."

"No, sir. I'm single and between relationships."

A scowl crossed the older man's worn face. "Well, what exactly *is* your problem?" he asked testily.

Young Finch averted his eyes, like a child about to confess some transgression. "The truth is . . . uh . . . the elevators are out of order, and I'm stranded down here. Do you know where the stairwell is?"

The Chairman's face reddened. "Down the hall and to the left," he said curtly. "You can't miss it."

As the visitor was leaving, he pointed to the clock in the corner of the office. "Nifty timepiece," he said. "Where did you get it?"

The Chairman smiled wistfully. "It was the clock we put in the lobby when I first joined the Firm," he replied. "The Board gave it to me when I retired. Replaced it with that silly digital wall clock!"

The young man glanced at his watch, then laughed. "Well, I suggest you get someone to take a look at that thing. My watch says it's five-fifteen."

After his visitor had left, the Chairman got up, grabbed his cane and hobbled over to the clock. "To Our Founder and Chairman," read the inscription on the side. "In Recognition of His Forty Years of Service." The pendulum was still, the hands stuck at five. He pounded his fist against the glass, to no avail.

"Infernal thing needs a new battery!" he muttered as he wearily donned his overcoat, turned out the lights and trudged out the door.

THE END

Books by Charles Rechlin

Riverdale Chronicles--Charles F. Rechlin (2003). Life, living and character studies in the setting of the Riverdale Golf Club by Charles F. Rechlin 5½ X 8¼, 100 pp ISBN: 1-888725-84-2 $14.95 MacroPrintBooks™ edition (2003) 16 pt. 8¼X6½, 16 pt, 350 pp ISBN: 1-888725-85-0 $24.95

Winners and Losers--Charles F. Rechlin (2005). a collection of humorous short stories portraying misadventures of attorneys, stock brokers, and others in the Urban workplace.
ISBN 1-59630-002-7 BeachHouse Books Edition $14.95 ISBN 1-59630-003-5 MacroPrintBooks Edition (large print) $24.95

Order form			
Item	Each	Quantity	Amount
Missouri (only) sales tax 6.925%			
Priority Shipping			$5.00
	Total		
Ship to Name:			
Address:			
City State Zip:			

www.beachhousebooks.com

BeachHouse Books

PO Box 7151
  Chesterfield, MO 63006-7151
(636) 394-4950
www.beachhousebooks.com

Made in the USA
Charleston, SC
23 April 2012